# CHAMPION OF DUSK & DAWN

Champion of Dusk & Dawn
Champions 2
By Megan Derr

Published by Megan Derr



Edited by Samantha M. Derr
Cover designed by Natasha Snow



First Edition June 2022

Printed in the United States of America

# CHAMPION
## OF DUSK & DAWN
### CHAMPIONS BOOK TWO

# MEGAN DERR

# CHAPTER ONE

Leonine had managed to make good time for most of the day, despite the weather doing everything in its power to thwart him, but by the time he reached his destination he was ready to fall over and sleep for a week. Nothing took the wind right out of you like doing even the simplest task in the freezing cold.

Why couldn't the assassins have waited until warm weather to do this? Surely that would have been easier on them as well? Then again, the sooner the world was rid of His Majesty, the better. His daughter hadn't even been officially coronated yet, and she was already leagues better.

The royal guards who'd initially been sent out to investigate the shots had come back with very little, unable to do more than flag the area they believed the shooter had used to fire the shots. It was a good distance away from the fairgrounds, meaning the killer was no trifle with a bow. Not the kind of person Leonine was enjoying hunting, but he would do his best. Hopefully he got the bastard before an arrow found his back.

From the shooting point, he'd followed what frustratingly little trail remained of a single horse riding quickly away. A large horse, used more often for farm work and the like, not one of the types used by knights and mercenaries.

It had taken him hours, and a lot of wrong turns and retracing his steps, before he finally came upon the faint remains of a campsite nearly two hours away, though a lot of that was simply the damned weather. That was a lot of traveling for such a quick, short job. Then again, he'd succeeded at murdering a king and getting away with it—so far.

Securing his horse nearby, but well out of the way of where he needed to search, Leonine slogged through the snow back to the small area that still showed signs of having been cleared to make a halfway decent camp. Whoever it was had even gone to the trouble of building a shelter from the snow, so they'd likely been here for a few days.

How had they known the duel had been moved forward, though? It had taken Leonine hours to get here from the cliff. There was no way someone could have learned of the changes all the way out here and then rushed to the cliff in time to take the shot.

But two or three people taking shifts… that would make sense. Three, likely. Kill teams were usually just a pair, but such a high profile target and the cold weather… twelve hours shifts would be nigh impossible, but three people on an eight hour rotation… One to watch the target, one to stand duty at camp, one to rest… possibly even a fourth, to relay information from town.

This wasn't just a crime of opportunity, someone who saw a chance in the tournament and went for it. This was an expensive, well-thought out and executed hit. His Majesty had always been intended to die during the frost fair. The challenge had changed some details, but that was all.

Interesting that the killers hadn't done it sooner. There'd been far better opportunities, countless cleaner shots, well before the duel. Why had they waited until then? Too many possibilities, impossible to narrow down at the moment.

He continued to scour the campsite, but they'd cleared it well. He couldn't even find bones left over from a meal. The remains of the fire had been thoroughly scattered, anything useful that might have been in it destroyed. Whoever the killers were, they knew their business. Increasingly, it seemed likely they were funded by wealth—nobility. Unfortunately, that didn't much narrow down the options.

Leonine sighed and sat down on a fallen tree, likely something the killers had done as well, given it made a perfect seat, close to where the fire had been, off the cold ground…

He braced his elbows on his knees and rested his chin on his folded hands, staring out over the campsite and the woods beyond. Nothing was exactly what he'd expected to find, but it was still frustrating. Something, anything at all, would give him a direction to work with when he reached Tesser City, which was his likeliest chance of finding information. If there was information to be found in the royal castle or city, the royal guards would have already found it.

Taking a deep breath, Leonine let it out slowly, watching the way his breath clouded around him. His lungs didn't love the cold air, but it was good for clearing the head. Sort of. Unfortunately, when he wasn't thinking about hunting killers, his stupid head took that as indication to turn back to his broken heart.

Everard, how big and warm and secure he was, friendly and congenial, how he seldom found fault with anyone. Odilia, soft and stern all at once, with the world's most beautiful smile. Together they were something else again, a small, loving family of two that took care of everyone who walked through their doors.

Leonine had spent his whole life alone, always at the fringes of everyone else's lives. Until Cimar had taken him in, accepted and mentored him, called him friend. It was all Leonine had ever wanted.

Or thought he'd wanted, until he'd caught the eye of a handsome, intriguing couple and been invited into their bed. Everyone knew they did that from time to time. Leonine had never thought he'd be one of the lucky few, though. He certainly never thought he'd be a delightful exception, the only person they invited more than once, the only one to become a regular presence, to stay the whole night through, one after another, until he'd lost count of them.

Fool that he was, he'd allowed himself to feel and want and wish for more. He'd even believed he'd gotten it when they'd said they'd come to the tournament to support Cimar, and by extension Leonine… He'd been so excited to invite them to his knighting, that soon he'd be a proper knight, standing on his own, with money enough…

For things that would no longer be. Because he was *too much* yet again.

Too much for his parents, who didn't need yet another child, let alone such a loud, active disruptive one who was ill-suited to farm life. Too much for the people who'd agreed to foster him, and instead dumped him at an orphanage before leaving with a pretty, tractable girl who better suited their lifestyle.

Too much for the orphanage, who didn't know what to do with him and his peculiar 'tricks' that were just early, untutored magic. Too much for all the potential parents that came by, who sought quiet, obedient children who'd be perfectly happy making shoes or working in a shop or making nails all day.

By the time he was eight and had run off to

join the military because it seemed to be the only place that wouldn't throw him out, he'd learned that he was too much of everything, and therefore not enough of anything.

Even in the military, a lonely child who just wanted friends and a place to belong, all he seemed to do was drive people away. Too noisy. Too active. Too smart. Too brash. Too flirty. Never mind his magic, which everyone seemed afraid of. It had taken him years to realize it was because he had more of it than was typical, could do things that people only heard about in stories, read of in books.

Cimar had been the only one to take him exactly as he was, and not just that, but *encourage* him. Leonine had finally started to feel like he was enough after all, even if he didn't really have any other friends, nothing more than drinking buddies and the occasional acquaintance or passing stranger to share a bed with.

Then he'd been invited to join Everard and Odilia… and invited back, and then to come whenever he wanted, to stay the night. They'd been everything he'd never known he'd wanted. He'd felt, really and truly, like he'd found where he belonged. The people who thought he was exactly the right amount of all the right things.

Fool him.

No matter how hard he tried, how hard he worked, at the end of the day, he was always going to be the wrong things.

Stupid, stupid, stupid. Now was not the time. He had more important things to do than sulk and whine about his failed relationship. If he even got to call it that, when he'd clearly never been more than an especially nice bed warmer. Gods, he really was as dumb as rocks, to think there'd ever been something deeper there.

Wiping his eyes, Leonine pushed off the log—and stopped as his feet shifted the snow and revealed a flash of gold. He crouched down and brushed snow away, until he could scoop the object up. He wiped remaining bits of snow away with his thumb and finally got a good look at it.

A charm, the kind woven into hair, this one shaped like a rearing horse. He bit it gently, and sure enough, it was pure gold. What sort of assassin went around with pure gold charms in their hair? The cocky sort, that was the answer. At least one part of the kill team was a cocky bastard. Good. Those weren't generally hard to find. Leonine rose and tucked the charm away in one of his pouches as he strode back to his horse.

He had enough daylight left he could keep going for a bit, especially since now that he'd reached the woods, there would be better cover from all the snow and wind. Mounting up, he heeled the horse into motion, mind already spinning plans for what he'd do once he reached Tesser.

A good, hot meal was first on his list, followed by proper rest. As much as he wanted to go straight to the hunt, rushing into it ill-prepared would help nothing. Cimar had always emphasized starting with food and rest whenever possible for as long as Leonine had known him.

Venison stew, that would be ideal, loaded with meat and potatoes and vegetables just the right softness, with thick, warm bread to sop up the gravy. Or roasted pork with an herb crust served with roasted apples and spicy greens. Rich mulled wine or a heavily spiced beer, tureens of creamy soup, fresh bread with butter and honey, sweetmeats and sharp cheese served with a fruity liquor…

His stomach growled in protest at the uncalled for torment, and Leonine sighed. If he was really lucky here in the next couple of hours, he might get to have wild hare for dinner. More likely, it would be the dried stuff in his bags and a cup or two of tea.

He should reach Tesser in a few days. In good weather, it took about three days of hard travel by horse, four or five at a more leisurely pace. As it was, he'd be lucky if he made it in less than six. The woods were providing reasonable shelter for the moment, but he'd be leaving them behind in a few more hours. Well, morning. He had every intention of camping in the woods for the night. No way was he sleeping out in the open before he had to, just forget that.

Gods above, he was tired. It felt like he'd had no real rest, even though he had managed to sleep a few hours before heading out. Ever since…

Leonine pinched his eyes shut to fight off the pain and tears. Dwelling and sulking and crying wasn't going to help anything. He'd been spurned. So what. It happened to everyone. Rejection hadn't killed him yet, it wasn't likely to kill him this time, no matter how much it felt like there were knives permanently lodged in his chest.

It was his own stupid fault anyway, for being too excited that last night to sleep well, drinking too much and trying to have fun, even if he didn't really have any proper friends in the castle. He'd also counted on the fun and eventual sleep he'd get after going to tell Everard and Odilia about his knighting and invite them to the official ceremony. He'd been so confident, so stupidly arrogant in his presumptions on the 'reward' he'd get from them…

Well, he'd gotten what he deserved for making such arrogant presumptions.

Movement caught his eye, and he brought up his bow immediately, pulling an arrow from the sheath attached to his saddle and letting fly as the hare spooked and cross his path. At least he wouldn't be eating jerky for dinner now.

Leonine stopped his horse, dismounted, and went to fetch his kill. He drew his knife and dressed the hare quickly, then affixed it to his saddle before mounting again. His mood wasn't completely improved, but damn it, he certainly wasn't as sour as he'd been just a few minutes ago. This was meat aplenty for dinner and breakfast, and if—

A scream of unbridled terror cut through the woods, and all thoughts of food fled. The scream came again, and Leonine heeled his horse into a gallop, rushing down the road. If the problem was anything, it was bandits, and they were especially nasty in winter, when travelers were scarce and food that much harder to come by.

Just as he was beginning to fear he'd have to risk going off the road to find the problem, he rounded a bend and saw them. Two travelers, man and woman, and four bandits, swords out, clearly ready to kill.

Leonine drew his bow again and fired rapidly. Never an easy or reliable thing to do from a charging horse, but he managed to hit two of them and cause general mayhem, which was all he needed.

Reaching them, he swapped bow for sword and cut down the two injured ones, one right after the other, leaving large splashes of blood across the snow.

The other two bandits were bolting for the trees. Leonine swung out of his saddle, grabbed his bow again, and fired, one, two, and three when the second arrow missed as the bastard unexpectedly ducked. As they fell, he swapped back to his sword and stormed across the field to finish the job. One simply needed to be put out of his misery. The other made a feeble attempt to fight back, and collapsed with a dying plea into the snow, his guts spilling out as he went.

Cleaning his sword, Leonine turned away to head back to the victims, eyes skimming for any lingering problems. There were no horses, but that was hardly surprising; horses were expensive, and bandits lived from one theft to the next.

Satisfied the threat had been dealt with, he finally turned his attention to the victims. "Have either of you been—"

He stopped, heart dropping into his stomach as he stared at Everard and Odilia. No. No, no, no *no*. That wasn't *fair*. They never traveled further than the city market if they could help it. What in the hells were they doing here?

"Sir Leonine!" Odilia said, looking like she was about to step forward, then stopping.

Sir Leonine. The words were another slap in the face. They were so done with him that they wouldn't call him Lee anymore. Just full formality. Like he was a stranger. Like he was nobody to them.

Too much and never enough, that was him. Well, fine, two could play that game. Three. Whatever.

"Master Innskeep, good Mistress. Have either of you taken injury?" Even as he asked, he finally registered that Odilia was in fact wounded.

It looked like she'd thrown up her arm to protect against a swing, and it had given her a pretty good slice.

Fuck, he should have noticed that immediately. Sheathing his sword, Leonine strode over to his horse and dug out the healing kit. Returning to the pair, he said, "Sit!"

Odilia obeyed, moving to a log that had been drug over to one of the fire pits scattered around the field, which was a well-known campsite for people traveling between the two cities.

Leonine knelt in front of her, removing his heavy leather gloves, leaving only the fingerless wool ones beneath them, and unrolled the healer's kit. He gently took her arm, feeling sick at heart all the while that he was so close, so fucking close, and yet oceans away and always would be now.

First he pulled out a bottle of alcohol, clear and flavorless, a trick he'd learned as a boy from a woman who'd cleaned up the scrapes he'd acquired getting into one fight or another. "This will hurt, but it will help prevent infection." When she nodded, he dumped the alcohol across the wound, at the same time feeding magic into her to mitigate the pain somewhat. He couldn't stop it entirely, his magic wasn't really inclined that way, but it did seem to help a bit.

When that was done, he corked the bottle and set to cleaning away blood, alcohol, and anything else that didn't belong. Once that was done, and the bleeding had slowed enough, he pulled out needle and thread. Moving to sit beside her, he settled her arm in his lap, across his cape so it wasn't resting on his cold leathers, and with a bit more pain-dulling magic, set to stitching the wound shut.

Throughout, nobody spoke, not even Everard, who could always talk.

Though the stitching took only moments, it seemed to last for hours. After he was finally finished, Leonine applied a salve and bandaged the wound, then cut away her ruined sleeve and used the clean, untorn section to serve as additional protective wrapping. "There. Keep it dry and change the dressing twice a day, and you'll be fine."

"Thank you, L— Sir Leonine."

Leonine tucked away his supplies and rolled the bag up again, tying it deftly before standing. Then he finally put his full attention on the pair. "What in the name of the goddess are you two doing all the way the hells out here? Have you lost your fucking minds? What's so damned important that it couldn't wait until spring?"

"My mother died, and I have to settle her accounts and collect her belongings before the end of the month, or the landlord will sell it all off and send out debt collectors," Odilia said, eyes on the ground. "We apologize for troubling you with our problems, good knight."

He wanted to *scream*. So they didn't love

him the way he'd loved them. Fine. That was his own stupid fault. But he hadn't thought they were so fucking indifferent to their time together that they were happy to treat him like a stranger now. Somehow, that hurt even more than the initial rejection. Despite every kiss, every laugh, every shared moment… he was a stranger now.

Too much of all the wrong things. Never enough of whatever it was people were looking for.

"I'm sorry for your loss, mistress," he said. "What is your destination?"

"Tesser," Everard said. "We didn't want to risk it, but we don't know what kind of mess her mother left behind, and we'd rather not let it build and find it even worse come the thaw. We'd rather be at home, believe me."

Of course they were headed to Tesser. Leonine had stupidly hoped that maybe they were heading for a nearby farm, one of the tiny, nameless villages scattered all over the countryside. He should have known he wouldn't be that lucky.

He had one chance to avoid the absolute misery staring him down. "I am headed to Tesser. I can speak with this landlord and convince him to learn a little patience, have everything put in storage for you, so that you can return safely home."

"I thank you for the gracious offer, sir knight," Odilia replied, "but I'm sure you are attending important business and should not be troubled with our trifles. You've already done enough for us."

Sir knight. Trifles. Like he'd never really mattered to them for a single moment. Had they ever meant a single word or action of the past months? Had Leonine been the only infatuated fool the whole time? He'd been so certain the answer was no, especially after they said they'd come to his knighting ceremony.

Now, the bitter taste in the back of his throat, the way his heart felt pierced by a thousand thorns, said the answer was yes, and he was a fucking fool for not realizing it until too damn late. He'd been caught up in a fantasy of belonging, of being wanted—even loved, though they'd never actually said any such thing—and reality had beaten that right out of him. Served him right. "Yes, I suppose I have. Even the most talented whore is only amusing for so long, after all. Fine. Whatever you want. As a knight of the realm, however, I am honor-bound to see you safely reach your destination, especially as we are bound for the same place. I suggest you prepare your camp for the night. I caught a hare earlier; that should suffice us for dinner."

He didn't wait for their reply, simply headed off back to his horse to get started on settling in for the night, half hoping he'd slip and break his neck and would no longer have to deal with this whole miserable fucking mess.

# CHAPTER TWO

After he took care of his horse, Leonine set to work piling up suitable branches from evergreen trees to form a rough bed. He rolled his spare cloak out over it, then laid out his bedroll and set his saddlebags in front of it, arranging his saddle to use as a makeshift pillow. All told, it wouldn't be a terrible place to sleep. He'd certainly endured worse.

With that attended to, he turned to make a fire—only to find Everard had that well in hand, along with an impressive array of supplies and equipment for cooking. It was leagues better than Leonine's barebones cooking set and single, lonely tin of powdery dried herbs.

Everard looked up, but then immediately back down, fussing needlessly with the fire that was already crackling nicely. "I can attend the hare if you like."

"By all means," Leonine replied, and handed it over. He wasn't so stubborn and prideful he'd subject them all to his cooking, which was passable at best, and more often best described as disastrous. He was much happier when all he had to do was enjoy the results.

Leaving Everard to the cooking, ignoring the thorns in his chest and the rocks in his stomach, he strode off to deal with the bodies, dragging each one deeper into the woods, where hungry animals would make quick work of them. He examined each for anything that might identify them, but came up only with a smattering of coin, a rather handsome knife he tucked away in his cloak, and a wool shirt on one that must have been stolen, as the quality was far too fine to have been purchased.

Returning to camp, he gave the shirt to Odilia before striding off once more to clean up.

When he finished, officially concluding his chores for the evening, he sat on his makeshift bed and bent to remove his spurs. He nearly started crying as he looked at them lying in his hands, large and heavy, beautifully made, *bejeweled* even. He had no idea what manner of jewel could look purple one moment and orange the next, but he loved it.

Tucking them carefully away in his saddlebags, he then dealt with all his weapons, putting them away or near to hand. Unfortunately, after that he ran out of things to do. If he were alone, he would simply fix his food and go to sleep.

With Everard cooking, however, dinner would be some time yet. Odilia sat close to him, the two of them occasionally exchanging looks, some silent conversation that Leonine would never be privy too. He and Cimar could converse like that. It had always made him feel special, to know someone that well, to be known that well.

They were both still hopelessly beautiful. Odilia's skin was just a slightly darker brown than Leonine's, with red undertones rather than his yellow. Her eyes were the prettiest shade of amber, her dark brown hair a mass of tight curls that she usually had up while working, but always wore loose otherwise. He'd heard some bar patrons call her mean, but he'd never known her to be anything but fair, stern at worst, and most often far kinder than people deserved. He loved her smile best, the way it filled her whole face, lit up her eyes and filled the room with sunshine.

Everard was built large, the sort of person who could lob problematic drunks from the inn with seemingly no effort. He was also as pretty as a painting, with really pale brown skin and black hair just barely tinged with gray, though he was barely thirty-five years old. He had smoky gray-blue eyes, and a laugh that could drive off even the foulest mood.

Like any regular of the Gold Cock, Leonine had talked to them plenty of times, flirting casually as he did with everyone. The first night Everard had sat with him for a bit during dinner, he hadn't thought much of it. As he, and Odilia, had done it more often, individually and then together…

He'd scarcely been able to believe his luck. Surely it wasn't what it seemed like? It had been, though, and better than he ever could have imagined. The only thing better than all the sex had been the first time they'd asked him to stay the night, when he'd slept right there between them, warm and sated and so happy he could have burst.

After that, every moment he could spare he'd spent with them, flirting and talking, helping around the inn… always ending the night in their bed. He'd started to think he was part of that *their*, even as he tried to remind himself that was not what they'd wanted. Even if they treated him differently from all their other lovers.

They'd called him Lee, and fucked him, and made him a regular part of their lives…

Now he was Sir Leonine and had to watch as they had silent conversations about him, like he was a troublesome customer they didn't want to risk offending.

Leonine rose, desperate to be anywhere but there, so close and so far away. He strode off back into the woods, fighting tears the whole way. Pathetic. After a lifetime of reminders that he was never good enough to keep, he should be long past tears. He had Cimar, a good life in the royal palace. He was trusted by the queen herself, for goodness sake. And, he kept forgetting because it all seemed so unreal, he had been granted land.

Good land, fertile and prospering, that would keep him in all the funds he could ever need for the rest of his life, so long as he was smart about it.

Yet he would give every last bit of that up, surrender it in a moment with zero regret, if Everard and Odilia said they hadn't meant it, that they loved him, and wanted him back, that he belonged with them.

Pathetic really was the only word for him.

He wiped his eyes with the back of one hand and looked around the woods, as though they might provide some answer to his life, or at least some relief from the wound tearing him apart from the inside out. There was only snow and rustling trees, though, and the distant call of birds.

Would he ever be good enough for someone? He'd liked being one of three, but he wasn't stupid enough to think he'd ever have that again. He was a knight, though, and close to the throne, with land and money now. That was suitable, wasn't it? That would finally make him enough of the right things.

Especially when he returned home having caught the assassins. He hadn't really thought about that before but having that triumph to his name would put him in high standing with the throne, the court. He'd be granted boons and honorable standing—and at only twenty-four, nearly twenty-five. If that wasn't good enough for someone to give him a second look, a chance… what was?

He'd come so far, so young. He was a good knight, a strong mage, and now he was also wealthy. He could dance, he could converse and flirt… Written out, listed so tidily, he sounded promising, right? Like he would be enough for anyone.

Yes, that was the key. He needed to stop moping, stop crying pathetically over people who didn't want him, had clearly never really wanted him past what he could do in bed, and focus on his task. Find the assassins. Return home victorious.

Cimar would tell him to believe in himself, that in the end his opinion of himself was all that mattered, was all that could make him or break him. So he would. He did.

If only believing it was as easy as telling himself to believe it.

Grit his teeth, make sure they all got safely to Tesser, see Odilia and Everard to their destination, and then it was back to work. Good plan.

Stifling a sigh, he paused to relieve himself and then finally headed back to camp.

Everard and Odilia were sitting close together, heads bents as they spoke quietly. Hopefully they weren't going to do something stupid, like leave in the dead of night. They'd just get themselves killed trying that. Every year people died because of poor choices made while traveling.

Leonine returned to his spot and, lacking anything better to do, pulled out his sword to ensure it was thoroughly clean. Being made of lindworm, it was just this side of indestructible, but nothing was immune to poor maintenance.

"That's not your usual sword," Everard said.

"No, it's not," Leonine replied bitingly, not bothering to look up. "It's a gift from Cimar on earning my spurs."

Neither of them replied, though Leonine supposed there wasn't much they could say that wouldn't sound woefully insincere, especially given that his job and the dangers therein were why they'd ended the relationship.

No matter how many times he reminded himself of that, though, it left a bad taste in his mouth. Chafed like badly fitted armor. Something about it didn't ring true.

Which only left that they preferred that excuse to the truth, that it was an easier escape for them. Which, in turn, meant the real reason was something they knew would be far more upsetting. That they'd grown bored, or his ways had shifted from amusing and bearable to unbearably annoying.

He should have known better. Odilia was thirty-one, Everard thirty-five. They'd been married since they were his age. He was seven to eleven years younger than them. What had he thought he could ever offer such an established, happy couple other than a few nights of fun? Even if a few nights had turned into weeks, into months.

All he'd ever had to offer was his body, and a warm, eager body was easy to replace.

Sheathing his sword with a touch more force than necessary, he set it aside and went through his saddlebags for any possible distraction.

All he turned up was the hair charm he'd found earlier. Sitting up again, he turned it over and over in his fingers, brow furrowing as he examined it more closely than he had before, searching for even the tiniest clue.

Unfortunately, there wasn't much to remark. The craftsmanship was excellent, meticulous and highly detailed, but there was no stamp anywhere on it to tell him who that craftsman was. That was highly unusual. Either it was made by some amateur craftsman for a friend or family member, in which case such a thing hadn't even been thought of, the craftsman was so well-known where it was made that a signature stamp wasn't necessary, or it had been removed, by time or intent. Any of the three possibilities was equally viable.

"Curse this fading light," Everard muttered.

Most of his attention still on the charm,

Leonine loosely cupped his right hand and called up his magic. It was a warm rush through his blood, sparks along his spine and then down his arm, coalescing into a marble-sized ball of moonglow light. He willed it brighter, bigger, until it was nearly double the size of his fist and a much mellower yellow in color.

Another pulse of magic, of will, and it rose to float above them, adding a much stronger light than that provided by the flickering flames. He wouldn't be able to leave it up long, but hopefully long enough for Everard to do whatever it was he needed.

His best bet would be to start with goldsmiths. He didn't know how many there were in Tesser, but the royal city, Katalar, only boasted seven, so there couldn't be more than that give Tesser was smaller. The craftsmanship would narrow it further. He should also…

The shift in the silence struck him then. Leonine looked up and found Everard and Odilia staring at him. "What?"

"How…" Odilia asked, eyes moving to the light. "I've never seen any mage do something like that."

"I practiced a long, long time. My apologies, I did not mean to make you uncomfortable." He closed his right hand into a tight fist, and the light vanished like a snuffed candle.

"No!" Odilia said, her crushed face just

visible in the firelight. When had it gotten so dark? No wonder he couldn't see much of the charm. "It's amazing. I knew you could do magic, L—but I had no idea you were so… so…"

"Spooky?" Leonine asked bitterly.

"Incredible," Odilia said, and he swore for a moment she sounded close to tears.

Leonine didn't reply. He didn't know how. That wasn't what he'd expected her to say.

"Dinner is ready," Everard said gruffly, in that way of his that said he was trying to keep the peace, even as he didn't really know how.

It was going to be a long week.

He accepted the steaming bowl Everard held out, stomach growling. How the man had created such a fragrant meal with just a campfire and a couple of hours, Leonine didn't know, but as ever, he was happy to enjoy the results. The hare was crispy on the outside, soft and juicy inside, richly flavored with spicy-sweet herbs. The bowl also contained turnips and turnip greens.

The meal was leagues better than the half-burned, half-raw hare that Leonine would have managed on his own. He definitely didn't know how to go digging up wild winter turnips. "Your food is delicious as always, Master Innskeep. Thank you."

Everard nodded and murmured a thank you, but he looked so miserable that it seemed Leonine had insulted rather than complimented him. Whatever. He gathered the used dishes and took them to clean, leaving them to dry by the fire before he went and sprawled on his bed, bundling up in his blanket and cloak.

What had he done wrong? What had he been too much of? Not enough of? He'd tried so hard, harder than he'd tried anything else, even training to be a knight, even his magic.

Nothing about the situation felt right. He should be over there with them, together in a warm pile that even this bitter cold couldn't best. He should be kissing them, checking them over thoroughly to insure they were well, that no injury from the stupid bandits had escaped his notice. He should be part of them, not over here alone and miserable.

Except he was far more acquainted with being alone than being part of anything.

Stifling a sigh, he pinched his eyes shut and tried to sleep. Thankfully, after the arduous day he'd had, and the lack of sleep preceding that, sleep came with relative ease.

He woke a short time later, though, at least to judge by the moonlight and the fact he was still exhausted. What had woken him? He reached reflexively for his sword as he sat up and looked around.

Everard and Odilia were missing. Where had they gone? Why had they left the safety of the camp? At least their belongings were still here; they hadn't tried to sneak away like he'd half-feared earlier.

Rolling to his feet, wrapping his cloak around him to ward off the miserable chill but keeping his sword arm clear, he summoned an orb of light and followed the tracks into the tree line.

He found them a few minutes later, huddled together close, speaking softly so their voices wouldn't carry—and Odilia was definitely crying.

"It doesn't feel like the right thing," Odilia said, as Everard rubbed her arms and drew her into a hug. "It feels—"

"I know," Everard said gruffly. "We'll get through this, just like we've gotten through every other hardship that's come our way."

They must be talking about something to do with Odilia's mother. Why come all the way out here to talk about it? What was the right thing that didn't feel right?

No, he needed to stop. Their problems weren't his problems anymore, except for getting them to Tesser alive and in one piece.

Sheathing his sword, vindictively pleased when the sound made them startle and cry out, he strode up to them. "I don't know what you two think you're doing, but it doesn't matter, because the only thing you're actually doing is being *stupid.* You're both old enough to know you don't go wandering about the woods at night. Get your asses back to camp and do not fucking leave it again, do you understand me?"

"Y-yes, Sir Leonine," Everard said, staring at him with wide eyes. "Our apologies, we needed to speak but did not want to risk waking you."

"Well, you did anyway," Leonine snapped. "Now move." He waited until they'd started walking and then fell in behind them, one hand resting on the hilt of his sword the whole while, eyes skimming for lurking dangers.

Back at camp, the pair immediately returned to their bed. Leonine attended the fire, ensuring it would burn the rest of the night, and then returned to his own bed.

One miserable night down. Too many still to go.

# CHAPTER THREE

Four days later, Leonine almost wished that horrifying lindworm Sir Cimar had faced just weeks ago had killed him. Even eaten by a lindworm, paralyzed and slowly rotting away in its stomach, would surely be better than spending one more interminable, tension-soaked day with his former lovers.

The tense silences. The shared looks that made him feel more like an outsider than ever. The way he could not escape it, not unless he abandoned them, which he absolutely would not do.

It would be so much more bearable if he had something to *do*, but travel was most often a boring business. Alone, he could have traveled faster, practiced his magic and swordsmanship… As it was, he was duty bound to protect, and despite everything, *wanted* to protect them, but that meant he could not turn his attention to things that would have helped to pass the time.

Instead, he brooded over the hair charm that was all he had to work with, searching in vain for any clue he might have missed. Unfortunately, there simply wasn't anything to find. It was quality gold, but utterly plain.

"What is that, if I might ask, Sir Leonine?" Odilia asked. "You keep looking at it so intently, and I know it's not my concern, but you seem troubled."

Leonine looked up, biting back all the angry words that wanted out at their tiresome formality. "It's a hair charm I found while hunting down the people I seek. All that remained at their camp. I'm bound for Tesser to see if someone there can tell me more about it."

Odilia hesitated, then said, "My mother worked for a goldsmith all her life. I might be able to tell you something, by your pleasure, Sir—"

"Stop acting like we're strangers!" Leonine snarled. "I know you turned me out, I know we're no longer—anything. Must you insult me further by acting and speaking like you don't even know me?"

"He said we didn't have the right any longer, to address you informally," Everard said. "Sir Cimar, I mean."

Leonine groaned and pressed his curled hands to his temple. "Damn it, Cimar."

Everard sighed. "Lee… if you are at liberty to share, what *are* you doing all the way out here? You're newly knighted. Shouldn't you be at home celebrating?"

"King Rorlen was assassinated. I've been ordered to find his killers and bring them home, one way or another. That is not information I should be sharing, so keep it to yourselves, please."

"We'd never betray your trust," Odilia replied. "May I see the charm?"

Not pointing out how badly they *had* betrayed his trust in them by throwing him out the moment one real obstacle appeared in their path, Leonine handed over the charm. Goddess knew he was sick of looking at the damn thing.

After a couple of minutes, Odilia said, "This is an apprentice charm. An excellent one, so probably an apprentice that has since been promoted to journeyman or will be very soon. I wouldn't be surprised if this was a test piece he then sold or gave away. There's no marks because legally such a piece can't be sold with a stamp."

"That is immensely helpful, thank you," Leonine said, aching that he could not his express his gratitude the way he once would have, kissing her breathless, so she drew back flushed and ever so slightly mussed.

He took the charm back and tucked it away, already shifting his plans to work with this new bit of information.

As Everard finished putting out the fire and burying it so there was no chance of embers escaping, he said gruffly, "Shall we resume?"

Leonine whistled for his horse, and helped Odilia up onto it, and Everard took up the reins to walk alongside them as Leonine walked on the opposite side, ready for any threats. The situation was not helped at all by the fact his horse knew Odilia and Everard well and liked them immensely.

They traveled in the same interminable silence that made every minute feel like an hour, and every hour like a day.

"Sir— I mean, Lee—"

Leonine looked up at Odilia, who was staring at him with far more misery than seem warranted, considering they were the ones who'd thrown him out. Shouldn't they be awkward but not miserable? He was starting to think he didn't know up from down anymore. "What?" he finally asked. "You can still talk to me. I know I'm the very last person you want to see right now, but I'm not going to remove your heads for wanting to talk. I just want you to stop acting like I'm a stranger."

Odilia looked near to tears again, but only nodded and said, "I only wanted to say a proper congratulations on winning your spurs. You deserve them, more than anyone I've ever known."

"Thank you," Leonine said quietly, his misery compounding yet again. He'd vastly prefer the congratulations they would have once given him: making him his favorite foods, eating with him in their private rooms, sharing a pitcher of their best wine. Dragging him to bed, where the best part was falling asleep between them and waking up in the same place. "I was also awarded lands. They belonged to the man Sir Cimar killed in the duel, after he attempted to cheat to win. They should have gone to Cimar, but he insisted I have them." He bit his tongue against rambling further, even though every part of him ached to impress them, tempt them, draw them back to him.

He could offer wealth now. Land. Stability. Acclaim. He could offer everything that people always wanted.

Their faces though, full of tension and misery, said that everything still wasn't enough.

He fell back into the miserable silence—but they hadn't gone more than a few paces when he heard voices. Laughter, complaining, something about needing to find food.

The back of his neck prickled. Cimar always told him to trust his gut, so that was what Leonine did. "Remember how I said to stop calling me Sir Leonine?" When they nodded, he continued, "Go back to doing that. For all the world, be two random travelers I saved and am escorting to Tesser. Give no indication you know me better than that, no matter what. Understood?"

"Yes, Sir Leonine," they chorused, voices thick with confusion.

"If anyone asks about me, especially when I'm not around…"

"We work at an inn, Lee," Everard said, amused and annoyed. "We know how to field questions."

"Right. Sorry. I'm tracking assassins, and it's put me on edge."

Odilia seemed like her old self for a moment, amused and fond, but it was gone in the next moment. "Do you really think…"

"I think anything is possible, and I think it's strange we've managed to catch up to travelers who must have had a significant head start on us, unless they're traveling this way, which seems unlikely this time of year. I guess we'll know soon."

They fell silent again, but this time it wasn't as miserable, just the tension of anticipation, of wondering and fearing what might come next. He could only imagine how much more they hated him now, being put in danger because of him a second time, when the first time was the reason they'd discarded him.

A couple of minutes later, they came upon the source of the voices, sitting on the side of the road cheerfully bickering. Well, one was sitting, their left leg crudely wrapped, and the other was standing, sword drawn, looking antsy despite the bickering.

They fell silent, gazes sharpening at the sound of newcomers—and their gazes sharpened further, all the way to suspicion, when they took in Leonine.

Mercenaries, both. One was long and lean, sharp as the blade he held, especially those cheekbones. He had long, dark blond hair pulled back in a messy braid and multiple scars on his face, dark eyes and surprisingly pale brows. His armor was good quality leather but showed signs of extensive repair. He also had arrows at his hip and an unstrung bow attached to the pack he wore on his back. His sword belt had a handful of pouches and two daggers, and his boots were the kind that could hold knives, likely for throwing.

The wounded man was kitted out much the same, though his armor was in better condition, and his bow was still strung. Unfortunately, neither had arrows that matched those which had killed Rorlen. Not that such a minor detail meant much; only a fool would make such a careless mistake.

Where the first man had white skin, unusual for the region, the second one had the far more common brown skin, his hair a dark brown-red falling in heavy locs down his back and over his shoulders. It was threaded heavily with charms, made from bone, wood, precious metals, and more. Several featured horses in some way.

Could it be so simple? Life was often strange, but it was rarely this easy. He'd have to bide his time, search things out—and wait until they reached Tesser, and Odilia and Everard would be safe, instead of caught in the middle and used against him. Again.

He smiled congenially, putting every bit of the flirt he knew how to be into it. "G'day, gentlefolk. Looks like you've hit a spot of trouble. Any assistance we can offer?"

"That's kind coming from a knight," the seated man said, quelling the standing one, who looked ready to wave them off. "Was hunting for dinner and accidentally interrupted a wyrm. It managed to get my legs with its spikes before we got well away. If any of you is a hand with healing, I'd appreciate it. We can pay for the trouble."

"I'm sworn to help, and happy to do so," Leonine replied. He drew his healing kit from his saddlebags, then approached them in the little clearing just off the road and knelt by the wounded man. "I am Sir Leonine of Darting, faithful knight of Her Majesty the Queen. Who be you, good strangers?"

"I'm Edger," the wounded man replied. Pointing a thumb at the other man, he said, "That's Cole. We're mercenaries out of Stone-by-Green, headed home after a job."

"Pleasure," Leonine said, stripping away the crude bandaging and propping Edger's leg back on the stump he'd braced it on to keep out of the snow. Opening his kit, he pulled out the tincture, thread, and needle he needed to properly tend the wound. He also used a bare thread of magic to ease some of the pain and start the healing, exactly as he had with Odilia.

When he was done, he drew back and used the snow to give his hands a rough cleaning until he could get to running water. "There, should be all set. Let me know if the pain or anything worsens. Climb on the horse with milady, and you can travel with us the rest of the day at least, and we'll eat together. Are you bound for Tesser at present?"

"Aye," said Cole, finally speaking, no less wary now than he'd been at the start. "It's a good place to stop, and it will take a couple of days for the clumsy knave here to heal up. We thank you, sir knight, for your assistance. What brings a noble knight of the court all way out here?" His eyes flicked to Odilia and Everard, who very clearly were not nobility, meaning it was unlikely Leonine was serving as formal escort.

"Queen's business," Leonine replied with a smile. "Nothing interesting, but I'm not at liberty to discuss it anyway. I met these two on the journey being attacked by bandits. Much like you, I tended milady's wound and offered to accompany them the rest of the way to Tesser. Perhaps now we're a merry band, we'll encounter no more ill tidings."

"Let's hope," Edger replied. "We are grateful. We'll do what dwe can to help secure dinner for tonight."

Cole helped him up into the saddle, settled behind Odilia, who looked like she'd rather walk, even though her skirts would make slogging through the snow especially miserable and difficult. He spared her a brief, sympathetic look, but didn't dare do more than that for fear their new companions might glean more than they should.

At least things were no longer miserably quiet. Cole seemed disinclined to talk, but Edger was more than happy to do so, flirting and chatting as easily as Leonine. Once upon a time, Leonine would have enjoyed himself immensely, been more than happy to see what flirting might lead to.

Right now, however, he really just wanted the whole mess over with, so he could go back to licking his wounds. Worse, Odilia and Everard watched and listened the whole time, probably more certain than ever in their decision to get rid of him.

"What about you, my fine mistress?" Edger asked. "What brings you out into such miserable weather?"

"My mother died. I'm headed to attend her affairs."

Edger winced. "My apologies and condolences. It's hard, losing a parent. Losing anyone, but some bonds cut deeper than others."

"We weren't close, but thank you, good sir. I'm fortunate to have my fine husband with me. If not for him, I would have fared quite poorly on this journey."

"Should get you some proper leggings," Edger said. "My sister always wears them in the winter months when she has to walk through the snow. Boots, leggings, dresses 'like a right man' everyone complains, but it's sure easier than all those heavy layers."

Leonine had never heard of a worse idea in his life. Odilia in leggings was *terrible*. He'd *never* get anything else done ever again if she walked around like that.

From the strangled noise he made, Everard agreed completely. "No, I forbid it. Not happening. Ever."

Leonine didn't have to look to see the look on Odilia's face as she replied, "I'll wear whatever I like, and you've no say in the matter. Wish I'd thought of it on my own."

It took every bit of self-control Leonine possessed not to whimper and moan at the images now in his head. At how delightful it would be to push her up against a wall, slip his hands into her leggings, push his fingers…

With an effort, he returned to his nonsensical chatting and flirting. "Forget women in leggings. I once spent a whole night with a man who looked a perfect dream in skirts. Just the skirts, mind. Nothing else."

Edger laughed. "Marvelous! Cole, we should put you in skirts sometime. Your hips could manage it, surely."

"My fist is going to manage your face if you don't stop acting the fool," Cole snapped.

"All right, all right." Edger rolled his eyes.

Cole made a frustrated noise, like a low

growl at the back of his throat, and abruptly peeled off from the group. "I'm going hunting. I assume we'll be stopping at the pond?"

"Aye," Leonine replied. "Seems a good place to break for the night, especially with those clouds coming up fast."

"I'll meet you there with dinner then," Cole replied, and slipped away into the woods before anyone could reply.

Edger rolled his eyes again and cast Leonine an apologetic smile. "Sorry for him. He don't mean nothing by it. He's always on edge after a job, before we have the money, and he never learned how to interact with people properly. Thinks I run my mouth too much, which is probably true, but he doesn't run his at all." He winked, and Leonine smiled despite himself.

"I know a bit about that. People always think I'm too loud, too talkative, too slutty—too much of everything, really."

Edger laughed, the sound wry and bitter and worn. "Yet somehow never enough."

Leonine felt like he'd been slapped. He looked up, caught Edger's understanding gaze. "Yes, exactly."

"Lucky me, I found Cole. He grumbles, but he puts up with me."

"I'm glad," Leonine replied. "Maybe someday I'll be so lucky."

"A handsome knight who helps complete strangers and claims the Darting lands? You'll be drowning in invitations!"

Leonine laughed. "I doubt it but thank you." He didn't look at Odilia and Everard, because if he did, he'd fall apart completely. Their ringing silence seemed answer enough. He didn't want to see in their faces that they were glad to be rid of him and his too much. They were probably desperate for this discussion to be over.

To be well away from him and this nightmare of a journey.

One more day's travel, and they could all part ways again. He'd once more be focused solely on hunting assassins, which was infinitely easier than spending hours with his ex-lovers. Especially given he was certain Edger and Cole were at least two of the assassins he sought. What a shame they seemed like such good people otherwise.

Around them, the snow that had been teasing all day began to fall, spurred on by a wind cold enough to slice to the bone.

# CHAPTER FOUR

The weather continued to be miserable the remainder of the journey and seemed to grow even worse as they stood waiting to be let into Tesser city. Thankfully, when the guards finally spied Leonine, they immediately waved him and his party through, more than happy to accommodate a royal knight and make their own lives easier in the process.

"Thanks," Edger said cheerfully as they paused in the pavilion. "Usually we have to answer five hundred questions about our business here. Traveling with one of you fancy types is handy."

"I'm honored to be of service," Leonine said with a laugh. "Where are the two of you off to, then?"

"Find a cheap place to sleep for the night, and then we're off again in the morning."

"Surely you're not in such a rush. What about your leg? Didn't you say you'd spend a couple of days here resting?"

Edger shrugged. "I've been doing all right so far, and healers ain't cheap. Not around here, anyway. Thanks to you, I'll be right as rain soon enough. If you're ever in Kormer and feeling lonely, look us up." He rested a hand on Leonine's shoulder and leaned in to kiss his cheek. "It's been a pleasure, knight." He kissed Leonine's other cheek. "That's a thank you from Cole." He waved to Everard and Odilia, who looked like they'd just drunk soured wine, and then the two were off, quickly lost to the milling crowd, as gone as abruptly as they'd appeared.

He'd have to track them down again later, but that shouldn't be hard. If nothing else, the only way in or out of the city was the gate, and the pair had no reason to sneak away, so he could catch them in the morning. He still wasn't entirely certain they were his assassins, though he'd tried and tried to pry any information at all from them.

"By all means, go after them if you like," Odilia said bitterly. "We hardly need your escort anymore."

Leonine snapped his attention to them. "What? I said I'd escort you to your landlord, and I meant it."

"Looks like you've better things to do with your time."

Anger sparked to life as he finally registered why they were scowling, why Odilia was speaking so horribly. "You're the ones who threw *me* out," he snapped. "You're the ones who decided I was too much trouble to continue bothering with. You don't get to be angry that I'm flirting with other people. You might also recall that I have good reason to think they're the ones I'm hunting, so it serves me well to keep them convinced I see them as harmless enough to flirt with."

Odilia's mouth flattened, and her eyes were still dark with unhappiness, but she only gave a terse nod and turned away. Everard met his gaze a beat longer, looking only tired and sad.

Stifling an urge to scream, Leonine took the reins of his horse back from Everard and motioned for them to fall in behind Odilia. Whether they liked or not, he was going to see this through. Duty first, above all else.

"Shall we find a room first, in case all this takes more time and effort than we anticipate?" Leonine asked. He wouldn't mind the chance to clean up and refresh, get his horse stabled, so she could rest as well.

They nodded, Everard muttering, "Whatever you wish."

Stifling a sigh, Leonine took over the lead, his spurs and horse good at clearing a path and making the way far easier.

He settled at the Orange Basket, a favorite stop of his and Cimar's when they'd worked for the monastery, protecting books and other important items the monastery made and brewed and grew.

As they knew him, it took several minutes to get past questions, congratulations, and idle chatter, but eventually he was able to escape, leading Everard and Odilia up to the room he and Cimar always rented when they were here, unless there was a rare occasion it wasn't available.

He set his bags on the chest at the foot of one of the two beds, then set to work on his armor. He didn't have full plate yet, as a proper knight would, but only because there'd been no time to commission it, everything had happened so quickly. Something to look forward to when he got home.

For the present, he sat at the bare end of the chest and removed his spurs, then his boots, then worked his way from top to bottom on his mail and the leather armor that supplemented it. Though the weight had been properly dispersed, it was still nice to be out of it for a bit.

He stretched with a long groan, then pulled his hair out of the knot he'd kept it in, combing roughly through the sweaty, dirty strands.

The soft sounds of swearing, the shuffling of restless feet, reminded him he wasn't alone. Once just days ago, he'd have stripped down in front of them without thought. Now, the idea made his stomach curdle. Why? What did it matter? It didn't.

He couldn't bring himself to do it, anyway.

"Sorry," he said. "If you don't mind, I'd like to bathe and get fresh clothes on, and then we can head out. I'm sure you're eager to have this done." So saying, he slipped behind the screen on the far side of the room, stripped down, and filled the tub there from a clever piping system that carried hot water from wherever they stored and heated it.

Though he would have loved to linger, soak in the heat until it began to fade, there were things to do. People to see for hopefully the last time, save in passing, though the idea of never really seeing Odilia and Everard again tore him apart.

Whatever. He was a knight trusted by the queen herself, risen all the way from unwanted orphan. He had made it this far; he would keep going. Someday, he'd find someone who wanted him forever.

The words were cold comfort to his broken and battered heart, but they were the best he had for the moment.

Climbing out of the water, he dried off with one of the cloths hanging on the wall and returned to his bags, where he swiftly pulled out the clothes he should have remembered to take with him. "Water is still warm."

Everard and Odilia only nodded, mumbled thanks without ever quite looking at him, and hastened behind the screen. Sighing, Leonine pulled on his clean clothes, bound his hair back in a small queue, and sat down to clean his boots as best he could before pulling them back on. After that, he worked on his armor, though he went with just the leathers for this trip, instead of pulling his mail back on.

Food arrived just as he finished, and by the time the others reappeared, he had laid it out on the table. They ate in silence, tense and miserable. He wondered why they kept enduring him, when it was so painfully clear they couldn't wait to be rid of him. They could have snuck off while he was bathing or something. It wasn't like he could have dressed and found them before they were long gone.

So why hadn't they? Maybe it simply hadn't occurred to them.

"Shall we?" he asked when they ran out of food.

"Yes, and thank you," Everard said. "I admit, what I've heard about this man from Odilia over the years, I'm not looking forward to dealing with him. We don't expect you to, of course, but your presence might mitigate the worst of him."

"We should be so lucky," Odilia muttered, and pulled up her cloak as they headed back out into the frigid day. "We're bound for Apple Street."

Leonine gestured. "Lead the way." He kept pace right behind them, making it clear he was with them. He'd have stood out significantly more if he'd brought his horse along, but the spurs were enough to draw notice and clear a path. So strange that it was *his* spurs provoking the reaction and not Cimar's.

Apple Street proved to be more of a rundown alleyway than an actual street, with rickety houses that stood up only because of the way they leaned into each other for support. The people milling about were in about the same condition, most of them too thin, with sickly, ashen skin, a few with the eyes of those who lived solely on cheap booze. A few people, mostly children or people so underfed it was hard to tell their age, begged for coins. Leonine handed out what he could, until they at last came to a stop in front of a house that was moderately nicer than the others, with an expensive lock on the door and bars on the window that said the owner had a regular problem with thieves.

"This is where you grew up?" Leonine asked.

"Not for all of it," Odilia said. "We started out better than this. My mom liked her liquor too much; in the end, she liked it more than her children." She pounded on the door, every bit the fierce queen who kept order in a rowdy tavern. "Mack! I'm here! Come out now, you slimy good for nothing!"

A couple of minutes later, after much turning of locks and rattling of chains, the door swung open, and a mean who looked exactly the way Leonine expected a slimy, weaselly, good for nothing slum lord to look filled the doorway. He looked like a corpse even starving vultures wouldn't touch, his facial hair so filthy that rats wouldn't use it for a nest. "Ah, Odilia, how I've missed your—"

"Shut the fuck up," Odilia said. "I'm here, as ordered. Let's settle up, so I never have to see you again."

Smile oily and sharp, Mack pulled a crinkled scrap of dirty paper from his jacket and held it out. "Outstanding debts and fees for care of the body."

Odilia snatched it from his hand, read it over, and then stared coldly at him. "I'm going to need to see proof of all of this."

"That's your proof right there," Mack said.

"This is your shitty handwriting making things up," Odilia replied, and threw it in his face. "Show me proof of debts my mother owed, or I'm not paying a single damned thing."

Mack laughed, cold and mean. "Go ahead, refuse. I'll have the sheriff summoned, and we'll tend this right off."

"Go ahead," Leonine said, stepping forward, the rattle of his spurs drawing Mack's attention, his eyes widening briefly before narrowing again. "Summon the sheriff. Even if he is your friend, as seems obvious, he'll be hard-pressed not to act as befitting his station in front of a royal knight, especially a knight who reports directly to Her Majesty the Queen and is currently on a quest by her direct command. Angering me is angering Her Majesty, and these are my friends, so go ahead and summon your good friend the sheriff."

Mack stared at him, perusing him slowly

up and down like he probably did his whores. "You're no royal knight. You're barely out of the nursery, boy. Did you steal your daddy's spurs to play big man for the little woman here?"

Leonine stared silently until Mack faltered, then replied, "I am Sir Leonine of Darting, formerly squired to Sir Cimar of Vallion, who is Victor of Challenge and Royal Champion to Her Royal Majesty Queen Korena Highrow and His Royal Majesty Prince Consort Davrin Highrow. His Majesty King Rorlen was assassinated six days ago. I'm sure by now you've heard the news, even with the abysmal weather. Do you really think Her Majesty is in the mood to hear that some worthless slumlord is harassing one of her knights while he is on quest by her direct and urgent command? Surrender your proof or withdraw your complaints."

Mack simply went back to sneering, but his darting eyes gave away his game, along with the jangle of cheap armor and cheaper weapons. Leonine sighed and as they moved to attack, threw his arms out and *pushed* his magic, filling the immediate area with blinding light. His would-be attackers screamed in surprise and pain, and Leonine set to work in earnest, getting rid of three of them before the light had entirely cleared. He rounded on the biggest one next, finally drawing his sword and buckler—

And barely dodging in time as the glint of silver caught his eye, and the sharp edge of a throwing knife sliced his cheek open instead of killing him. Snarling, Leonine ducked away from the big guy, turned, dropped his buckler, and threw his hand out, turning the snow beneath the knife-thrower's feet to pure ice, causing him to slip and hit the ground hard. The man went still, blood spilling in a steady pool around his head.

Turning back to the last one, Leonine summoned fire, cupped between his hands, hot and bright and deadly. "Stand down."

The man stared at the flames, at Leonine, and then turned and ran.

Leonine banished his magic, retrieved his buckler, and narrowed in on Mack, who tried to flee inside his fortress of a home, but didn't do it fast enough. Grabbing him up, Leonine shoved him against the wall and braced him there with one arm across his throat. "Let's try this again. Submit proof or drop your complaints. Which is it?"

"L-l-let me go!"

"Which is it?" Leonine hissed.

"Pay the burial costs! Just those!" Mack wailed.

Leonine withdrew enough that Mack could stand properly, but kept firm hold of his shirt. "Key to the house?"

Mack dug it out and handed it over with a trembling hand. Leonine took it and handed it off to Everard, then threw Mack to the ground and dropped a coin in front of him that would more than cover the burial costs. "Cause me or mine anymore trouble, and it will be the last decision you ever make. Are we clear?"

"Yes."

"Are we clear?" Leonine repeated icily.

"Yes, Sir Knight," Mack said, scrambling to his feet, covered in snow and mud and gods knew what else, slinking into his house and slamming the door.

Leonine jerked his head at Odilia. "Lead the way."

Odilia watched him for a moment, a look on her face that he simply couldn't parse, and then nodded and turned away, leading them a short distance down the street. The house was as derelict as the rest, but someone had attempted to grow flowers in the bare scrap of earth in front of it. Odilia stared at the flowers sadly a moment, and then unlocked the door and slipped inside.

"I'll stand watch," Leonine said. "Let me know if I need to have a cart or anything brought."

"Thank you, Lee," Everard said quietly, and looked for a moment like he might say something else, but only gave a sad smile and slipped inside, leaving Leonine alone.

Across the street, some people came up to deal with the men he'd wounded, dragging them away to… honestly, Leonine didn't know and didn't care. His cheek was sore and itchy where it had been cut, but past a quick pulse of magic to deal with the bleeding, he left it for the moment.

He sighed, keeping watch for any new threats, desperately trying to ignore the stares and whispers no doubt provoked by the magic he'd used in that stupid, pointless fight. Exhaustion washed over him, all the magic use after a long, hard day of travel and inner turmoil not helping anything. He ignored it. A few more hours and he'd be back in his room. He could lick his wounds, physical and otherwise, and get some sleep then. For the present, he still had a job to do.

Hours, however, proved to be minutes when Odilia re-emerged carrying an old, worn wooden jewelry case, Everard right behind her. Odilia continued walking across the street, where she spoke with an old woman who was feeding a handful of scraggly chickens and handed over the key and a few coins. She returned after a few minutes, looking even more exhausted than Leonine felt. "It's done. Thank you, Lee, for all your help. I can't imagine how much more difficult this would have been for Everard and I, even formidable as he can be."

Everard snorted. "I couldn't have dealt with six men like that, not armed and skilled as they were. I certainly didn't have magic to throw at them. You're amazing as ever, Lee."

"Then why wasn't I good enough to keep!" Leonine burst out, then swore, pressed the heel of his hand to his forehead, and fled.

# CHAPTER FIVE

He heard them call his name, but he didn't want to hear whatever they were going to say. He'd already heard it, and the wound wouldn't close, no matter how hard he tried. Maybe after this, Her Majesty would be willing to let him take some time away. It felt like from the moment Cimar had risen as Davrin's champion, they'd been going, going, going. From lindworm to race to attempted assassination to duel and all the fallout thereafter.

From cautiously happy with his lovers, to being tossed out. From squire to knight to wealthy landowner and sent out to hunt assassins before he could settle into any of it.

Now this.

He was just so *tired*.

At least this little side quest was over. He'd acted like a perfect fucking fool right at the end, but he'd fled before it got worse, and now it was over. Once this quest was over with, he wouldn't see them again, except in passing around the city, and hopefully he'd be too busy to go into the city much.

Right now, it was back to the task that had been entrusted to him.

First, though, he really needed to tend the cut on his cheek. It was going to scar, but he didn't need to make it worse. He paused at a public fountain to clean his face, so he didn't look so much like a mad terror running amuck in the city, and then got directions to the nearest healer.

An hour later, he was patched up and ready to go to bed, but his work was only beginning. Thankfully, the healer had given him the locations of the town's three goldsmiths. One was even close, and then he could swing by the inn and get his horse before heading for the two across town.

The air was only getting colder as the day went on, and would be well into deadly once dark fell, but there was nothing he could do about it. He'd get as far as he could today, and then sort out what to do tomorrow.

Do his best not to think about how damned lonely his life seemed suddenly.

Argh, whatever. He had been alone before and it hadn't killed him; he'd be just fine now too. Well, he'd be fine eventually. Especially now he didn't have to see Everard and Odilia again.

Pinching his eyes shut, he took several deep breaths, until the stabbing, twisting pain in his chest subsided. Opening his eyes again, he pressed on, more relieved than was warranted when the little sign for the goldsmith shop came into view.

The shop was surprisingly warm as he stepped in and closed the door. Rubbing his face to thaw it a bit, he approached the counter. On the other side of it, an old man slowly rose from a chair where he'd been working on some bit of jewelry and stiffly walked up to the counter. "Can I help you, young— Oh, sir knight, my pardon. What can I do for you?"

"You are Master Spyro?"

"I am."

"Thank you for your time. I am hoping to find where this might have been made. I know it's apprentice work, but I don't know where the work was done. Does it look familiar to you?"

Affixing a loupe to one eye, Spyro gingerly took up the hair charm and examined it. "I haven't had an apprentice for years now; the last one moved on to study in a larger city. Young folk, you know. She tended more toward insects and flowers. I never knew her to make animals. This particular style though, more stylistic and fanciful than accurate… you might try Jofferson."

"That's the one at Red Circle?"

"That's him," Spyro said with a smile that was polite and distracted. "Anything else I can do, Sir Knight?"

"No, thank you for your time," Leonine replied. "I appreciate the help. Good day."

Back out in the cold, he headed quickly for the inn, tense and irritable for no good reason.

Well, no, he had hoped this first stop would provide answers, and instead he was going to have to go all the way across town after all. By the time he got back, it would be well into dark. He just wanted *rest*.

Duty first, though. Reaching the inn, he paused long enough to grab a mug of hot cider before going to get his horse. By the time the stable hands had his horse ready, the cider was gone and Leonine was feeling moderately better.

He rode off, pulling up his cowl to ward off the worst of the miserable wind, setting the horse to an easy pace, so they wouldn't endanger pedestrians or spook any animals milling around, the usual assortment of chickens, goats, and other livestock brought in toward evening and when the weather was too miserable for grazing. He did not miss sharing sleeping space with goats.

The goldsmith on Red Circle had a handsome shop, nothing remotely like the sad little shack he'd visited first. Leonine was vastly more acquainted with the first type of shop, but technically he could now afford this second one quite easily. It was a strange thought that didn't feel quite real yet.

His chest gave a twisting ache as he thought of all the goods he would have happily bought for Odilia and Everard. Jewelry, fine fabrics, the best wines, horses, even a carriage… He would have given them anything. Everything. Still not enough.

Sighing, he tethered his horse to the post in front of the shop and headed inside.

Two clerks were at the counter, and behind it at the worktable were four figures bent over their work—three women and a man. At the very back, sitting behind a massive desk, was presumably the proprietor, a man nearly as big as the desk.

"Good afternoon, Sir Knight," one of the clerks greeted. "How may we be of service?"

"I need to speak with the proprietor on a matter of Queen's business, please," Leonine said. The clerk's eyes widened before he caught himself, and then he was gone, heading brisky but smoothly to the back of the room.

The proprietor rose and immediately headed for the counter. "I'm always honored to serve Her Majesty. What can I do?"

"Master Jofferson?" When he nodded, Leonine continued, "Would you look at this charm? I am attempting to find who made it, though I realize it's apprentice work and so pinning down an exact maker is difficult."

Jofferson snorted. "Not hardly. This is Spyro's work, from *our* apprentice days. You can see by this tiny 'X' here on the hoof. We aren't legally allowed to mark them for sale, but we had our own private little tells." He handed Leonine his loupe and pointed to a tiny mark on the front right hoof. "There."

Leonine looked, stones sinking into his

stomach, the back of his neck burning with anger and humiliation. "He said this was likely done by you."

"Spyro is a damned liar, and he's had a lot of practice," Jofferson said. "He worked here once, right alongside me, years and years ago. He was more interested in shoddy work and fleecing customers, though, so out he went. Guess he's still up to his old tricks."

"Damn it!" Leonine snatched up the charm and bolted, untethering his horse and heeling it to a fast pace, shouting for people to get out of his way as he raced back across the city.

When he reached Spyro's shop, he threw himself off his horse and into the shop.

He wasn't remotely surprised to find it empty, only that Spyro hadn't bothered to lock the door.

An old man couldn't have gotten too far, even with his significant lead.

Stupid, he was so *stupid*. Such an obvious, careless mistake, a child's trick and he'd fallen for it like a fool. Cimar would be ashamed of him.

Recrimination would have to wait. Leaping over the counter, he crossed to the door at the back of the shop and then up a set of creaky steps to the room above the shop.

Also empty, but showed signs someone had packed in haste. Multiple someones. The killers had been *here*. Leonine slammed his fist against the wall. *Damn it.*

Moving further into the room, he made a cursory search for anything useful, but only came up with a secret compartment in the floor that had been opened and never closed again. A stash. So Spyro and the killers had made a run for it, and had suitable funds to do so. Fuck.

Returning outside to his horse, Leonine swung up into the saddle and headed off. If they'd raided a stash and whatever they could hastily throw in a knapsack, they weren't planning on hiding in the city. Nor was it likely they'd double back to the royal city. No, they were headed further east, either northeast to the larger city there, or slightly more dead east to the large port city where ships were happy to take on last minute passengers, no questions asked, as long as the money was good.

Thankfully, they wouldn't have had time to reach the fork, so he didn't have to play that guessing game—yet.

He raced out of the town, ignoring the guards and others who called after him demanding answers, ignoring the wind slicing into his face, the snow that had begun to fall in earnest, the heavy clouds that promised the weather was not going to get better.

Nothing and no one would keep him from fixing his mistake. He would not return in disgrace, a failure on his first mission as a royal knight. How could he have been so—

Leonine cried out in pain as an arrow

struck his shoulder, causing him to jerk, startle his horse, which resulted in him flying out of the saddle and to the ground.

Vivid red splashed across the snow and grime. Snarling in pain and frustration, Leonine heaved to his feet and drew his sword. Four men came running at him, and Leonine cast out his magic, turning the snow to ice, sending them—

He jerked at the sound of running coming up behind him, just in time for a fist to slam into his face. Leonine went stumbling back, and another two were on him. Someone grabbed his wrist, snapped it, and Leonine screamed.

After that, he didn't remember anything.

*~*~*

He woke with a gasp, tried to sit up, and was immediately halted by a warm, heavy hand on his chest. Leonine shuddered and collapsed, staring up at the ceiling. The inn. How had he gotten back to the inn?

Turning his head, he stared into Everard's somber face. That made even less sense. They should be back at Odilia's old house, or headed home, or something. Not here. With him. "What are you doing here?"

"We went looking for you," Everard said. "After… after everything. Found your horse wandering the town center, scared and exhausted. He managed to lead us to you, don't know how. That's a good horse you've got, Lee. Saved your life."

Leonine swallowed. "I should hope so, given how much I paid for him." The joke felt flat. "Help me sit up. Is there anything to drink?"

"Got some tea here, though it's gone cold."

"It's fine." Leonine whimpered slightly as Everard gently helped him sit up. To judge by his headache, he'd undergone extensive healing, but there were some things only time could fix. "The bastards who got me, where are they?"

"Long gone, I'd imagine. Be careful, the healer fixed your wrist, but she said to use it minimally for a couple of weeks so strain doesn't undo her work."

Leonine grimaced and sipped at the cold tea. Chamomile and honey. Cheap and easy to come by. He'd drunk it a lot in the orphanage, all the other houses that had never wound up being home. It wasn't his favorite thing in the world, but it was familiar, and right then he really needed familiar. "Thank you for the help."

Everard snorted. "You paid for all of it; Odilia found your coins. We also ensured you'd have this room for as long as you needed it and arranged firewood and food aplenty. Horse is stabled and getting all the oats and carrots he could ever want."

"Thank you," Leonine replied. "You didn't have to do so much for me. I'm not your problem anymore." *You're not my problem anymore.* How many times had he heard those words growing up? Too many to count. He preferred not to think about it, but like any old wound, the ache was always there, especially when hard times stirred it up.

Anguish and shame filled Everard's face, and he reached out to brush Leonine's hair from his face, thumb tracing his cheek in a caress that Leonine had desperately missed. He wanted to scream for Everard not to touch him and beg for him to never stop.

"As to that… we were hoping to talk, Lee," Everard said with a soft sigh. "There's something we need to confess."

"Confess?" Leonine suddenly wished he was still unconscious. "How long have I been out?"

"Just a few hours, thankfully. Healer said if you didn't wake up by morning to fetch her again, but she said you'd probably wake up before dinner. Glad she was right." He dropped his hand and covered one of Leonine's with it. His hands were so big and warm, always a steadying presence, a strong and gentle touch Leonine had come to depend on. He'd fought so hard and long to be a knight, to be somebody that nobody could knock down—at least not easily.

It was still nice, though, when he could set his sword aside and rest, rely on someone else's strength for a little while. A weakness. A mistake. When would he ever learn?

He'd been so certain, though… confident enough to invite them to his knighting, to plan his future with them a major part of it. He'd been so *happy*.

Until he'd proven to be more trouble than he was worth. Again. Why had he been stupid enough to expect this time, this relationship, would be different?

He pressed the heel of his left hand to his forehead, wishing the headache would ease off. Wishing his stupid fucking thoughts would just *stop* for a little while. "Where's Odilia?"

"Went to get food, should be back shortly." Everard took the mug as Leonine emptied it. "Get some more rest, Lee. We'll be here when you wake up."

"I don't have time to lay around here. I need to go after those bastards. They were the assassins. I can't let them just get away. If I hadn't been so stupid—" He stopped as Everard's hand landed on his chest, holding him in place gently but firmly. "What?"

"Lee, you need *rest*, and even if you were in fighting shape, there's a blizzard raging outside. It's not safe to cross the street, let alone go chasing after *assassins*. If they're out there in this weather, they'll be lucky to survive the night. If you're really set on hying off after them, at least wait until the storm abates."

"Damn it." Leonine wanted to cry. He'd been played for a fool. Had been ambushed.

Nearly killed. He was supposed to be a knight, had been trained for years by Cimar, and the moment he was on his own, he was an incompetent buffoon who couldn't do anything right. The best training in the kingdom, years of practice… and still not enough. Never enough. "I think you're right," he choked out. "I should just go back to sleep."

"Lee…" Thankfully, Everard fell silent, though his hand remained on Leonine's as he settled down and closed his eyes.

What were they even doing here? Wasn't this one of the reasons they'd severed the relationship? Too much trouble, too much risk. What had Everard meant by something they needed to confess?

He faintly heard the door open, Odilia's soft voice, but exhaustion was winning out by that point, his eyelids too heavy to drag open, and he fell asleep wishing with every part of him that this wasn't some strange, temporary thing, that they'd always be…

*~*~*

When he woke again, it was to hazy morning light, like it was struggling to make a dent through the heavy clouds that persisted, at least to judge by the snow piled on the window ledge and the chilly room.

The fire had all but died down and… he

was alone. Had he imagined Everard? Probably. But then, who had helped him? Had he just been talking to himself last night, some fever dream? That certainly made more sense that Everard and Odilia helping him after he'd nearly gotten himself killed, when they'd thrown him out precisely because his life was too dangerous, not worth the risk.

Leonine drew a deep breath and let it out slowly, ignoring the twinges in his chest that spoke to bruised ribs. How many mercs had jumped him? At least… He pressed the heel of his hand to his head, willing back the lingering headache as he tried to think. Remember. One had shot him. Four had come at him directly. At least two had come from behind. One of them had snapped his wrist like a twig, which was alarming. Wrists didn't just snap like that. It took significant force and leverage.

He dropped his hand and stared at the wrist in question, wrapped in bandages that smelled potently of astringent herbs and had the faint soreness that came with fast, hard healing magic. Hopefully he'd be able to fully use it again. What good was he if, after all these years, he was suddenly useless as a knight? What was there left for him?

Whining and feeling sorry for himself certainly wouldn't get him anywhere, though. If he hadn't been doing that in the first place, he wouldn't have nearly gotten himself killed charging recklessly into danger.

Bracing himself, he pushed away the blankets and swung his feet over the edge of the bed. His whole body ached, like he'd been thrown down the side of a mountain, but it was bearable. For now, anyway. Taking another breath and bracing himself anew, he pushed off the bed and stood.

Standing. Progress. Where were his things? That question was immediately answered as he spied them across the room, his armor on a stand with the sword belt hooked over it. Next question: how was the weather?

He shuffled over to the nearest of the two windows in his room and glanced out. So much snow had fallen that it came halfway up the houses on the streets. People wouldn't even be able to open their doors.

Looked like he wasn't going anywhere. Wonderful. He'd as good as failed his mission. What was he supposed to do now? Lie around and succumb to further fever dreams of his ex-lovers returning?

Resting his forehead against the window frame, Leonine pinched his stinging eyes shut to ward off more stupid, pointless tears. He was young. His spurs weren't even a month old. It was the dead of winter. Nobody won a fight one against six—at least six. He was just exhausted and in pain and overwhelmed. He'd get through this.

He'd survived a lindworm for crying out loud, even if strictly speaking he hadn't done anything but run away on Cimar's order. After his own stupid clumsiness had woken the damned thing. He was lucky Cimar hadn't wrung his neck once it was all over.

Right. He was stuck inside for at least a few days, possibly several, given that the snow was still falling. If he couldn't move, his enemies couldn't move. So he'd focus on recovering and working out a plan.

Turning away from the window, he headed back to the bed, where he could see cold tea and a bottle of cheap brown glass that likely held a tonic to help with the pain, possibly even to speed healing, though such things were uncommon.

He hadn't made it more than halfway when the door flew open. Leonine tensed, braced for a fight—and stopped, arms falling to his sides as he took in Odilia, half-covered in snow, her face reddened by the wind. "What are you doing here?" Had he not dreamed it all after all?

"You! What are you doing out of bed!" Odilia said—then burst into tears and threw herself at him, nearly causing Leonine to topple before he caught himself.

He held her tightly, like he had so many times in the past, a bone-deep ache coursing through him. Movement caught his eye, and he looked up to watch as Everard closed the door and set down the bags he was carrying before retrieving the cord of wood Odilia had dropped and taking it over to build the fire back up.

Odilia just kept crying, holding on so tightly it was hurting his poor battered ribs. "I thought you were dead!"

"Well thanks to you I'm not," Leonine replied. "I wasn't expecting an ambush, though in retrospect, I probably should have. I'm glad you found me, though I still don't know why you're going to all this trouble. I thought trouble was precisely the reason you didn't want me anymore."

That set Odilia into a fresh burst of tears, head burrowed against his chest as she said, "We didn't mean it. We were trying— But it didn't— Then you almost died. You were so still and cold to the touch, and there was so much blood." She cried harder, and at a complete loss as to what to say or do, Leonine just held her.

He cast wide eyes to Everard, who looked nearly as miserable as Odilia. "What in the world is going on?"

"Let me go get some food while the fire warms this place up. Sorry it lapsed. We were helping the innkeep bring in more foodstuffs and supplies, and the weather caught us for a bit. Fire's going good now, though, and I'll get the food, and then if you're willing, we'd like to talk. You might not want us to stay when we're done, but we'd like a chance to explain ourselves, if you're willing."

This day got stranger and stranger. "All right."

Everard nodded ever so slightly, in thanks or acknowledgement Leonine couldn't say, and slipped away, leaving Leonine alone with a still-crying Odilia.

# CHAPTER SIX

"Odilia, it's all right. Whatever is wrong, we'll work it out. Don't cry yourself sick."

She nodded against his chest, but her tears eased only slightly, and she clung to him like he was a log in a stormy river.

"Come on," he said, more bemused with every passing second. He guided her to the bed and sat them on the edge of it—or tried to, anyway, but Odilia somehow wound up in his lap and wouldn't be budged.

It only worsened the ache in his chest, the longing that wouldn't abate no matter how much time passed, how clear they'd made it they didn't…

He didn't know what they wanted or didn't want anymore, and that was almost worse, because it provoked hope, and he wouldn't survive his hopes being crushed again. He'd thought he'd found everything he'd ever wanted with them, something more precious than even his hard-won spurs. Why would they suddenly change their mind after he proved to be an even more trouble?

The longer he waited, the less he wanted to hear this mysterious confession.

He had no idea how to help her right then, and that was worse, because he never wanted to see either of them in pain. Normally when Odilia was upset, if Everard couldn't get her to talk it out, Leonine was good at distracting her, getting her to eat or sleep, until she did reach the point she felt like talking. It always made him feel like he really belonged, had a place and purpose in their little trio. More fool him.

"Not like you to cry so much," he finally said. "They must have really done up my pretty face."

That got her to glare instead of cry. "They *did up* every last scrap of you, and it's not a joking matter."

"I'm a knight. This isn't the last time I'm going to get beat up. I'm fortunate you two were there to compensate for my reckless stupidity. I'll definitely be smarter going forward. I… wasn't as focused as I should have been, though I thought I was at the time."

"That's our fault too," Odilia said, sniffling again. "Oh, Lee, we've made a mess of everything, and we just wanted to do the right thing."

"The right thing? What in the world—" he broke off as the door opened, and Everard entered bearing not one but two trays of food. The smell of roasted chicken made Leonine's stomach growl. There was also bread, butter, cheese, stewed vegetables…

He couldn't forget that comment though. Pushing Odilia from his lap, he rose and said, "All right, I can't stand it anymore. What is all this about a confession? Doing the right thing? I'm tired of the mysteries. Do you hate me now or not?"

"No!" Everard and Odilia said together, so loudly every room on the hall probably heard them. Everard practically dumped the poor trays on the rickety table and then they were both crowding into his space. He loved it and hated it in equal measure, and hated himself for missing it so damned much.

"Lee, I'm so sorry. We're so sorry. We wanted to do the right thing and only made a complete fucking mess of it all." Everard reached out, hesitated, then let his hand fall. "Lee, we love you. We've loved you for a long time, and we never stopped."

"Then why did you cast me aside!" Leonine burst out. "I needed you, I *saved* you and you— I wasn't enough." His vision blurred, and he pressed the heels of his hands to his forehead. "Too much trouble and not enough of anything to be worth keeping, that's what I am. You threw me out like everyone else." He jerked back, turned to do something, though gods if he knew what.

He hadn't made it more than a step when Everard pulled him back, pull him close, against that large, warm chest, wrapped in those strong arms, right where he'd always thought he'd belonged, until they'd reminded him that nobody ever really wanted him. Not like this. Not forever.

"I don't understand what's going on," Leonine finally said, pulling away, hating himself for his stupid tears, for appearing so pathetic in front of his former lovers.

"You've never been too much trouble, Lee," Everard said quietly, the most somber Leonine had ever seen him. "We lied. We… we were ashamed we'd caused *you* so much trouble, that we were so easily overtaken and used against you and… we always knew *we* weren't good enough for *you.* We hesitated for weeks about approaching you, certain we weren't worthy of your time and attention."

Leonine stared at them, wide eyed and lost. "What?" That was the stupidest thing he'd ever heard.

"Sit down, Lee, before you fall over. Eat something," Odilia said, and before he could protest, muscled him into the closet chair and set a filled plate in front of him. "You're a knight. You're young. Beautiful. Highly sought-after and well-liked by everyone. It was clear to all of us that someday you'd marry into noble, or even royalty. Someone worthy of you. Why would you waste any of your time on a pair of old innkeepers? You did though," she added sadly, sniffling. "You did waste your time on us, as little of it as you had between training and helping Sir Cimar."

"It was never a waste," Leonine said, staring at his food but not remotely hungry anymore. "I'd watched you two for ages. I never thought you'd turn your attention to me, and never in my wildest imaginings did I think you'd invite me back over and over. It seemed completely reasonable that you finally got tired of me and didn't want to deal with being in danger because of me." It had been a stab through the heart, but reasonable.

"Lee..." Odilia threw herself into his lap again and clung like ivy, warm and soft, reassuring even as the whole situation left him floundering. "After— After those cretins tried to use us against you, it only reaffirmed for us that we weren't good enough. That we'd be a perpetual weakness to be used against you. You belonged with a duchess, or a prince, someone with money and resources, who was too powerful to be used against you, who could stand with you as an equal." She swallowed, forehead pressed against his, eyes pinched shut. "Someone who wouldn't hold you back. We also knew you wouldn't listen if we said all that, so... so..."

"So we lied and drove you away," Everard said. "It was the hardest thing we've ever done, and we regretted it before we'd even finished doing it. We still think you're too good for us, Lee, and our choices—the pain we've caused you— might be unforgiveable, but... we thought you were dead, lying there in the snow. There was so much blood." He covered his eyes, but tears escaped anyway. "I never want to see that again. Especially since I can't help but feel it was our fault, causing you additional turmoil when you needed to focus on your mission."

Leonine opened his mouth. Closed it. Repeated the movements. Words wouldn't come. He didn't even know how he felt. Angry? Hurt? Confused? Relieved? All of it and more. "You… you don't hate me? You don't think I'm too much and yet not enough?"

"No, Lee!" Odilia said, throwing her arms around his neck and holding him tight. "We love you. With all our hearts we love you and have only ever wanted what was best for you, even if that wasn't us. I still don't think we are, but would you give us a second chance anyway? I promise we'll do everything in our power to earn it."

"All I ever wanted was to be with the two of you. Why did you take my decision away from me? It wasn't your right to make my choices for me," Leonine finally managed. "I loved you. I risked everything for you. And you cast me aside for my own good?"

Everard's face fell, and until then, Leonine hadn't realized just how much hope had filled it. "We're sorry, truly. We know it was stupid and wrong. I don't know what to say, except that we foolishly thought we were doing the right thing. We wanted to help, and we did it the worst way possible. Is there anything at all we can do to fix this?"

"I don't—" Leonine stopped as Odilia started to slide from his lap. Slink, rather, like she was suddenly ashamed of herself for being there. It was the last thing he wanted though, still more distance between them all. He'd never wanted the distance in the first place. He was angry and hurt, and his pride wanted to tell them to get the fuck out, he didn't need people who were going to make such important decisions without having the decency to treat him like an equal in the matter...

But he didn't want them to go. He wanted Odilia right where she was, and Everard there with them. His pride wasn't more important than the two people who meant the most to him in the whole damned world.

Holding her tight, not letting her slink away, Leonine finally said, "Don't leave me again. Don't cast me aside. Not unless that's what you really want. If our relationship ends, then it ends, but don't end it because you're doing 'what's best for me,' that's not your right. You weren't a weakness in my eyes. If you'd bothered to talk to me like you should have, I'd have said you were my greatest source of strength, you stupid clods."

Letting out a cracked, broken noise, Odilia sank her fingers into his hair and dragged him into a kiss, mouth impatient and overeager, but so sorely and desperately missed that Leonine really didn't care about the details right then. He looped an arm around her shoulders and held her close, kissing back with equal fervor, all the cracks and crevices caused by their abandonment beginning slowly, very slowly, to fill.

When they finally broke apart, Odilia was scooped out of his lap and set on her feet, and then Leonine was pulled to his feet and swept up in Everard's arms. "We're sorry, Lee, with all our hearts, I swear to you we're sorry. If you'll give us one more chance, I promise we'll make this right, whatever it takes, however long it takes."

"Shut up and kiss me already."

Everard obeyed, and Leonine moaned as the cracks filled a little bit more, some of the bruising on his heart easing. They still wanted him. They *loved* him, which they'd never said before.

"So you'll give us another chance, Lee?" Odilia asked when Everard eventually set him on his feet. Leonine had missed how easily Everard could manhandle him.

Leonine wiped his face, still feeling foolish at all the crying he'd done lately. "Of course I will. I never wanted to leave your sides. Why did you have to make everything so needlessly complicated?"

"Don't ask me," Odilia said with a wobbly laugh. "I swear it made sense at the time, but hell if I know why. Can I have another kiss?"

Leonine obliged, dragging her in close and taking her mouth with the same feverish hunger he'd felt in their every encounter. He'd missed them so much. Everard treating him like he weighed nothing, Odilia soft and full in his arms, her breasts pressed to his chest in tantalizing tease and promise. Every deep groan and soft whimper, the gasps and breathy pleas.

Everard pressed up behind him, hands on his hips, mouth on his throat, sucking up a mark that Leonine would feel for days.

He swore when they withdrew abruptly. "No stopping. Why are you stopping? Don't do that."

"You're still recovering," Odilia said, "and you really need to eat. You won't recover your strength by us mauling you."

"No, I definitely want the mauling. *Need* the mauling," Leonine said. "After weeks of feeling—" like he would never be good enough for anyone to love him "—alone, believing that you hated me, I could really *really* do with a good mauling."

Everard rolled his eyes. "Stop calling it that, honestly you two."

Leonine laughed, a bit shaky but true. "Then get on with *it*."

"What are we, children?" Everard said with a sigh, even as he hauled Leonine in and cupped the back of his head. "It's called fucking, you can use that word, you're an adult. I should know, I've checked thoroughly."

That really set Leonine to laughing, even as

Everard kissed him again, pulling him flush against that big, strong body, leaving Leonine feeling small and almost fragile, a rarity between his training and his magic.

When they parted, Leonine was panting. "I never thought I'd get to do this again."

"Neither did we," Everard said, smiling sourly. "Especially given we were the fools who threw you away."

"Well, you fetched me back, so it works out," Leonine said. Trust didn't rebuild in a moment, but… this was a good start, and he understood their thinking, even if it was massively stupid thinking. "Now fuck me."

"Lee, you're in no shape—"

"You don't get to argue with me!" Leonine said.

Everard rolled his eyes, but the fondness in them, the smile twitching at his lips, said victory belonged to Leonine. Good. After weeks of feeling alone and abandoned, he desperately wanted to feel part of something again, and tangled together in a sweaty mess with these two was the best way to do that.

"Keep him warmed up," Everard said, setting Leonine back on his feet. "I'm going to do something about the beds."

Odilia immediately wrapped around him, kissing him ardently, one hand twined through his hair, the other sliding down to get a grip on his ass. "Missed you, Lee. Can't wait to see Eve buried inside you."

Leonine groaned, that and a hundred other delightful memories and images filled his head. Sadly, he was in no shape to try most of them, and even with Everard pushing the beds together, there wasn't proper room for the rest of them. "We can just use the floor."

"Far too cold for that, and you're battered enough, you goose," Odilia said with a laugh. She dragged her tongue across the mark Everard had left on his throat, setting it to throbbing again. Then she pulled away just enough to get his pants undone before sinking to her knees in a way that immediately set him moaning. Chuckling, she took hold of his cock and licked the tip teasingly, then along the length, until he was gasping and struggling to hold still.

Only then did she swallow his cock, taking him deep into her mouth, the back of her throat, cheeks hollowing as she sucked with a devastating expertise that never failed to leave Leonine feeling wrung out and well-used in the best possible way. "Odilia—" He spilled down her throat, the fastest he'd ever come, but unable to hold back after all the *too much* he'd been through the past few weeks.

He pulled gently out of her mouth, but before he could drag her back up to begin his own efforts at making *her* scream, he was grabbed from behind, spun, and all but thrown sideways across the two narrow beds that had been pushed together so that his head was against the wall, where Everard had moved the pillows.

Leonine had barely gotten himself righted and settled when Everard, naked and enormous, settled between his thighs. He bent and took Leonine's mouth, kissing him until he was panting and trembling, then set to work putting his mouth over what seemed to be every last bit of skin he could possibly reach.

Odilia climbed onto the bed and settled next to him, twisting open a small wooden jar he knew well, and not just because they used it often. He'd actually helped her make the contents before, on a rare day off. Eyes hot, she slicked her fingers and said, "Let's get you ready, hmm?"

"Oh, I'm ready," Leonine said on a groan as Everard's teeth sank into his hip, right in the spot that always made him shudder, his skin prickle as pure lust raced hot up his spine. His spent cock twitched, tried to rise to the occasion again.

Everard paused briefly in his efforts to kiss Odilia, and that was always his favorite sight, the way they kissed with a familiarity that only years of knowing each other in the most intimate ways could bring. He'd thought maybe someday he could be part of that with them… and then he'd lost it all… and now he wasn't sure he could quite believe it would happen again, but the little seed of hope was already growing.

Pulling away, Odilia nipped Everard's jaw and said, "Going to use that mouth on me when you're done with him?"

"Is there still breath in my body?"

Leonine moaned, thrusting restlessly, reaching for them. "Use my mouth."

"No, not this time," Odilia said, smile full of affection and mischief. "You're still healing. Don't worry though, darling knight, once you're properly healed up, I will avail myself. You know how much I enjoy sitting on your face."

He moaned again but forgot everything he wanted to say as her deft, slick fingers pushed inside him. He took two easily, her fingers long and slender. Only moments later, though, as he began to ride them, one of Everard's joined them. Leonine flailed helplessly for something to grip, hips jerking as he tried to get *more right now*, but he was prisoner to the pace they set, and their pace was excruciating. "More, damn it," he finally managed to gasp out, only to be met with a pair of smug, husky chuckles.

Odilia and Everard kissed again, then withdrew, and finally *finally* Everard was pushing inside him. Gods, he'd missed this: Everard stretching him wide, almost burning, filling him full. Odilia teasing, kissing, her skin flushed and glistening, mouth hungry and talented as she kissed him while Everard fucked him.

Too much. It was all delightfully too much, especially as Everard increased his pace, driving into him over and over, and Odilia's strong, but delicate hands wrapped around his cock, and everything sent him over the edge again, Odilia's mouth muffling his screams as he came apart in their arms.

When he could function again, it was to find himself sandwiched between them—just as it had always been, as though the past few weeks of misery where a nightmare. He tried to say something, maybe that he was simply happy to have them back, but sheer exhaustion caught up to him, and he fell asleep to the sound of them speaking quietly and someone stroking his hair.

# CHAPTER SEVEN

It took three days before the snow ceased falling, and another two before anything was remotely passable. Even now, staring out the window at the world of white he could easily step out onto from here, he clearly had a difficult time ahead of him.

Footsteps padded across the floor behind him, and then Odilia's head was resting on his shoulder, hair brushing his cheek as she sighed. "Sun's not even really up yet, and you're ready to go. Always our Knight of Dusk and Dawn."

"Your what?" Leonine asked with a laugh, dislodging her as he turned.

Odilia smiled. "That's what we call you: our Knight of Dusk and Dawn. Champion, maybe, given how often you've saved us now. Come to us after sunset and leave with the sunrise. We almost never get to see you during the daylight. Maybe now that will change."

"I hope so," Leonine said, covering her hand as she rested it against his cheek. "I'd like to see you both more, now that I'm not just your longest-running bit of entertainment."

Sighing softly, Odilia said, "You never were, right from the start. Wish we'd handled it better."

"You handled it just fine last night."

"Oh, shut up," Odilia said, playfully smacking his cheek before leaning in to kiss him. When they eventually drew apart, she said, "I wish you'd wait another day or two, but I can tell from your posture that you won't."

"I'm not going to fail my first mission," Leonine said. "I *can't.*"

"You won't," Everard said from the bed as he slowly untangled himself from the sheets and sat on the edge of the bed. He yawned hard enough that Leonine's jaw hurt watching, and then added, "Anyway, if you're this stuck while snug and safe and snug in the city, think how hard a time they've had out there in the wilderness. They'll be lucky if they're still alive."

"I guess I'll find out," Leonine said, and reluctantly nudged Odilia back so he could finish packing.

"Let us come with you," Odilia said. "In weather like this, better to be in a group."

Leonine shot her a look. "Absolutely not. I am not dragging civilians further into this mess. You've already been hurt twice dealing with bandits and that stupid slumlord. I can't protect the two of you and myself against professional killers."

"We're not completely helpless," Everard

said. "We know how to stay out of the way at any rate. Also, without us you'd be dead, so I really do think it's better if we come along for now."

"No, and that's final," Leonine said, shoving the last of his belongings in his saddle bags before he set to getting his armor on. When he was ready, he hefted his bags over his shoulder and turned to the door—and drew up short to see it was blocked by his lovers, their faces set. "I said no."

"We're your lovers, not your employers," Odilia said. "We don't have to obey you. Anyway, there's nothing you can do if we just happen to be traveling the same direction as you."

Leonine glared. "That's cheating. I want to know you're *safe*, damn it."

"We want to know *you're* safe," Everard replied quietly. "We found you two steps from death, Lee."

"You can't come with me every time I'm sent out on a mission. Danger is the nature of the job."

Odilia folded her arms across her chest. "Of course we can't go on every mission—but we can come on this one, and we're going to do so, and there's nothing you can do to stop us. The weather is miserable, you're still healing, we have no idea how long it will take to find and catch them, or how many there are. Maybe we can't fight, but we can support you."

It was abjectly stupid. Civilians shouldn't

get mixed up in such things. Cimar would kill him if and when he found out—but Leonine couldn't keep wasting time arguing, and they were right: there was absolutely nothing he could do if they decided to just follow along, short of employing methods that would be inappropriate on strangers, let alone his lovers. "Fine. Whatever. You're both stupid, and I'm not happy about this at all, though."

Everard grinned and reeled him in as Leonine got close enough to reach. He dragged a slow, tingly kiss across Leonine's mouth. "I'm sure we'll talk our way back out of trouble."

"I don't think 'talking' is what you have in mind," Leonine muttered against his mouth before taking a more thorough kiss. When he drew back, he was immediately turned to enjoy the same from Odilia. Goddess, he had missed them, this, so, so much. "Shall we be on our way then?"

"If you insist," Odilia said. "I still say more rest is the smarter idea."

"I want to get moving while we can, because otherwise we'll be here until spring." Leonine led the way out of the room and downstairs, where they found an impressively empty dining room, the innkeeper sitting at a table doing paperwork. "Any way out of here other than the upstairs windows?" Leonine asked.

Looking up, the innkeeper said, "We have a tunnel to the stables to tend the horses, and another to the road, but after that you're on your own."

"Appreciate all you've done," Leonine said, and flipped him a coin that would more than make up for all the lost business caused by the weather. "Do you have any horses to spare?"

The innkeeper flipped the coin and caught it. "Go ahead. If you can have them back by spring, great. If not, you've more than paid for them. Be careful out there, and you're welcome back anytime, sir knight and friends."

"Thank you. Be well." Leonine headed for and out the back door the innkeeper indicated, and walked through a tunnel of snow, as eerie as always for the dark and quiet, but familiar too, because he'd done the same thing many times going between house and shed with a family he'd lived with briefly.

In the stable, he let Everard ready his horse while he looked over the few that belonged to the inn, finally settling on two that looked spry enough for the journey and hardy enough for the weather. Once all three horses were set, they led them out to the street, where some of the way had been crudely cleared, and the rest most definitely had not.

The day was definitely going to be long and arduous. Thankfully, for the moment the world was still. Heavy clouds hung in the sky, and it was near impossible to tell the time of day, but the air wasn't as cold as it could have been, and the wind was mild.

"I'll keep watch for food," Everard said, "and places to stop, so you can focus on your mission."

Leonine smiled in thanks. He still didn't like them being out here, where they could all too easily take an arrow or get the nasty end of an ambush, but he couldn't deny he liked having company—especially theirs, now that all the turmoil between them was resolved.

He kept most of his attention on their surroundings, but he was highly unlikely to find anything until they were much further from town. "So I know you'll be too busy with the inn come spring, but later in the summer, if I'm not out on a mission, would you like to come visit my new holdings with me? Her Majesty will probably grant me time to settle into the role, see what needs to be fixed and the like after the likely neglect of my predecessor."

"Ooh, la, me traipsing about a castle like my lover owns it," Odilia said with a laugh, holding a hand to her chest. "Won't even know what to do with myself."

"I'm sure you'd find something," Everard drawled, "especially since I can already see Lee intends to drown you in fancy gowns and jewels and whatever else your magpie heart desires."

"What in the world would I do with all that nonsense? I can barely manage the three gowns I do own."

Leonine laughed. "It's a castle—there's staff for that. You're going to have to get used to the idea you're not the staff anymore, not when you're with me."

"Don't think they get out the gold candlesticks and the fancy plates for the lord's scandalous lovers."

"Scandalous?" Leonine scoffed. "What's scandalous? You should see what they get up to in the royal castle. Just days before I left, Lady Winra was caught with two footmen *and* her personal maid. All at once. In the same bed. Some are saying her husband almost killed her and sacked all of them, but others are saying he joined right in. I had to leave before I could figure out the truth, sadly."

Everard laughed. "You and your gossip."

"It's like free entertainment all day, every day," Leonine said. As long as he didn't take it seriously or actually judge anyone by it, as most gossip had all the substance of fairy candy. "There were rumors only just trickling in about Lord Caruther's newborn when I had to leave. Hopefully someone will catch me up on everything when I get back."

"There's always someone willing to talk about other people's problems, don't worry," Everard replied. "If not for free, then usually for a few drinks."

Leonine laughed. "Divine truth. I…" He trailed off as something caught his eye, a bit of root or something that seemed out of place. "Hold a moment." He guided his horse toward it, drawing his sword just to be safe—and immediately sheathed it again when he got close enough to see it was a boot, and that boot hadn't moved for some time.

Dismounting, Leonine dug out his trowel and set to clearing the snow away as best he could. After a few minutes, Everard joined him, and then it was quick work to finally get the body free.

"One of the men who attacked me," Leonine said. "Looks like he was heading for town to treat his wounds. Why didn't someone help him?" The snow he'd been buried in was caked with red, so he'd clearly bled out before he'd frozen to death, though the difference had probably been slight. "If he'd had help, he likely would have made it."

Everard pulled the body to a clearer, firmer patch, and with a quick kiss of thanks, Leonine crouched and started to go through the dead man's clothes. Easier said than done, since he was as frozen as the ground, but a careful use of magic made things a bit easier.

Unfortunately, his efforts didn't turn up much: coin, cigarettes, a couple days' rations, a cheap knife, and a smudgy charcoal drawing on a piece of greasy paper that looked like the kind herbs, medicines, and other such things were wrapped in at sale. "What is this, do you suppose?"

There really wasn't much to the drawing — some lines and numbers, one of them circled.

Everard took it. "Port map, I think. Dock nine. Place is a maze if you don't know it, so people are always drawing these little shorthand maps that can be matched to the official one at the port." He grinned and handed it back. "Surely you fancies need to get around the port too."

"They send servants, or simply go to the main office and send one of their staff to do all the hard work," Leonine said with an answering grin. "So assuming this is a recent thing, and not leftover from a previous job, they're heading for the port. That's something, at any rate. We'll need to work hard to catch up to them, though. If they reach the ship before I reach them…"

"You're vastly underestimating how much this weather is slowing down everyone who doesn't have your abilities, money, and determination," Odilia said with a smile. "Come on, unless there's more you can get from him." She wrinkled her nose, but like any innkeeper, she'd seen her share of the dead and dying.

Leonine and Everard mounted back up, and the trio rode off, making slow, but steady progress to the tree line, where hopefully things would get a bit easier.

"What I wouldn't give for a mug of tea right now," Odilia muttered. "When we stop for the night, I'm going to drink so much I'll be boiling clear through tomorrow."

Everard laughed. "You'll be pissing clear through tomorrow too."

"Oh, shut up," Odilia said as Leonine laughed. "You men and your latrine humor."

"I mean, he's right," Leonine said.

Odilia sighed.

As they entered the tree line, following the closest thing to a road he could find, the going did indeed get easier. Eventually they were even able to settle onto the actual road, which made traveling even easier.

Unfortunately, if the men he was hunting had made it into the tree line, they could be well on their way to the port by now, and there was no way Leonine could catch up in time, even if he was traveling alone.

"Stop worrying yourself to death, Lee," Everard said gruffly. "You don't know where they are, what's happened, what could be delaying them—too many variables to be worth obsessing over."

Odilia laughed. "You should know."

"Yes, exactly."

Leonine cast them a puzzled look. "What do you mean? I don't think Everard worries about *anything*. Except maybe when you both worried about me so much you cast me aside."

They both sighed. "We don't need the reminder."

"Too bad," Leonine replied in singsong tones, and laughed when they glared at him.

"Seriously, though, Everard never worries."

"Used to, though, when I was a little younger than you. Worried myself literally sick. Headaches, couldn't keep food down… had to work a long time to get over that habit. Every now and then it tries to creep back up, though less and less the older I get. By the time I'm wrinkled down to a prune, probably won't even worry about taking a shit."

Odilia groaned. "Stop it!"

Leonine and Everard laughed.

When they reached the eventual split in the road, which Leonine had been quietly worried they wouldn't, given how difficult it had been at times to follow the road—they veered left, toward the port city of Javera.

They hadn't been traveling down the new road long when Leonine heard something. He threw an arm out, halting the other two.

Just when he was starting to think he'd imagined it, or had simply heard an animal or breaking branch, the sound came again.

A sneeze. A poorly muffled, very human sneeze. Signaling the other two to remain where they were, Leonine slowly and quietly dismounted, drawing his sword before venturing off the road and into the woods where the sneeze had seemed to come from.

Several steps into the woods, he came across evidence of another person, and the further he went, the more obvious the signs became, especially the odd splashes of blood scattered about. Someone had been foraging about for food, but not long or well. Likely they were sick or injured.

Leonine pursed his lips. Injured. Like a man with a leg wound that had slowed him down before and might be proving an even greater trial now with the weather so much worse, especially if he hadn't been able to afford a healer.

Could it be Edger though? Seemed a stretch, except Edger and Cole had bothered him from the start, and it wouldn't surprise him at all to see them again, right in the middle of this mess. He still could make no sense of the larger image, but he felt strongly they would be right there in it.

He continued on, following the crude, careless trail until it ended at the entrance to a cave. Putting his fingers to his lips, he whistled for his horse. Next he held out his left hand and called up his magic, creating a ball of light that he sent on into the cave ahead of him. When it seemed there was no immediate danger, he went on ahead, calling the light back to hang just behind and above him.

The smells hit him first: the remains of a fire, burned meat, and blood.

"Should have fucking known it would be you," said a familiar voice.

Leonine relaxed slightly. "Edger. What are you doing at the back of a cave?"

"My stupid leg, what else?" Edger said, his

voice raspy, thin.

As Leonine drew close enough for the light to reach him, he immediately saw why: Edger was propped against the back wall of the cave, shivering, and his leg wound had gotten worse, not better. He also seemed to be holding his arm carefully, and he was far, far too pale. "Where's Cole?

"He had to keep going with the rest of them. Only way we'll get our money," Edger replied, mouth twisting. "Guessing your business is that the queen has sent you to take our heads."

Leonine sighed and enlarged the light, then crouched to examine the dregs of the fire. Edgar must have run out of wood. There was also the remains of a couple of squirrels. Grimacing, Leonine moved to address Edger, cupping hands over his wounded leg and pouring all the healing magic he could muster into it.

Not much, in the end, but from the way Edger's expression eased a bit, clearly it was better than nothing.

"Sorry, healing isn't my thing."

"Doesn't hurt as much, which is all that matters to me right now," Edger said. "Your magic is something else. Never seen one like you."

"Will you be all right for a few minutes while I fetch my companions, some wood, and real food?"

Edger laughed. "Will I be all right? Already better than I was, ain't I? Thanks for not killing me outright."

"I'm a knight, not a mercenary," Leonine replied, and stood, heading back out of the cave just as the other two came into view, following his horse with confused expressions. "Guess who I found?"

"To judge by your expression, I'm not going to like the answer. It better not be that pair of upstarts who *definitely* aren't allowed to flirt with you anymore," Odilia said, voice taking on the ominous tone of a barkeep who'd reached her limit with rowdy, drunken patrons.

Leonine laughed. "Half right. I'm going to collect firewood. Eve, would you see about catching a rabbit or something? Odilia, don't kill him while he's helpless."

"Fine," Odilia groused, and set to dealing with the horses as Leonine and Everard headed off into the woods.

# CHAPTER EIGHT

Thankfully, collecting firewood didn't take long. Leonine improvised a sling and carried as much as he possibly could on his back, and still more in his arms, trudging through the snow back to the cave, spurred on through the biting cold by thoughts of tea and food and not moving for a few hours.

He dropped the wood off, stole a quick kiss just because he could, then headed back out to forage suitable branches for beds, hauling them in bundles until he had a suitable stack by the door. Odilia came to help him then, dragging them into the cave and making the bed piles.

By the time he was finished, Leonine's body ached, and his lungs burned from the cold air. He still needed to actually make the beds and get water, but a few minutes to rest and warm up wouldn't hurt.

"That fire feels wonderful," he said with a groan. "Thank you, Odilia."

Odilia smiled faintly. "I'm going to see about water. No, sit, I can handle it just fine, you overprotective twit. You're more qualified to tend him, anyway. Back soon." She kissed him, took his waterskin along with her own, and headed off.

"I thought they seemed like a good deal more than strangers you met along the way," Edger said. "The way they glared whenever we flirted with you…" He laughed. "I was far more concerned what they were going to do to me than you."

Leonine rolled his eyes. "They weren't my lovers at the time. It's complicated. Let me have another look at that leg." He dug his healing kit out of his saddle bag and set to work, cleaning and re-stitching the wound, covering it heavily with salves for healing and numbing before carefully bandaging it, offering whatever additional healing he could muster. "Why didn't you go to the healer?"

"Complicated," Edger bit out. "Stupid, mostly. Let's just say that people wanted to talk to us, and they didn't feel like waiting, and then we were running for our lives." He laughed sourly. "Supposed to be an easy job. Shoot a stupid arrow or six, run away, collect our money, jump on a ship, and away we go." He sighed. "It's not like anyone actually misses the stupid bastard, not from all I've seen and heard." Leaning back against the wall, he closed his eyes and seemed to sink inward. "I hope Cole at least gets out of this mess. I don't want him dead because of my stupid decision to accept this job. Should have listened to him."

Stifling a sigh, Leonine set to work fixing up four beds, retrieving Edger's bedroll from where it was still rolled up beside his battered knapsack. Once the beds were ready, he helped Edger onto one, and wasn't remotely surprised when he passed out almost immediately, the tension in his face bleeding away.

Leonine's stomach churned. This man was one of the assassins he was supposed to capture or kill. Why did it feel like doing either of those things was the wrong action to take?

Whatever. A problem for later. He still needed to capture Cole, and ideally whoever was working with them.

When Odilia returned, he helped her with filling the kettle and getting a pot of gruel going. "How's our guest?" Odilia asked. "Prisoner?"

"Something," Leonine replied with a sigh. "Tired. In pain. Scared. Mostly for Cole, but also for himself."

Odilia gave him a sharp, pensive look filled with entirely too much knowing. "What's bothering you?"

"To be honest, I don't know yet. I need to find Cole and the others, get a better idea of the whole tapestry before I know what questions to ask, let alone the answers. I really do hope they're having as much trouble with this weather as we are."

"Trust me, with a group like that, the kind that would ditch one of their own..." Odilia's lips curled. "They're struggling with every step. The harder the journey, the more vital the cohesion." She rolled her eyes and smiled faintly, fondness in her eyes. "Which a well-trained knight would know."

"Never hurts to be reminded," Leonine replied, returning the smile. "Even if I still think you two stubborn brats should have stayed back at the inn."

Odilia laughed and fixed them all cups of tea, finishing just as Everard appeared with two freshly skinned and cleaned rabbits. Handing his cup to him, she took the rabbits and set to work butchering them, throwing most of the meat in the pot with the simmering gruel, bundling the rest together with string and carrying it outside where the cold would preserve it.

Leonine drank one cup of tea quickly and poured a second to linger over, enjoying the warmth seeping into his frozen fingers. Nearby, Edger still slept, snoring faintly, occasionally muttering or whimpering in his sleep, hands twitching as though he was reaching for something. Or someone.

"What do you make of all this?" Everard asked, nodding to Edger.

"No idea, to be honest. They're not exactly what comes to mind when you picture assassins. Hopefully once we find Cole and the others, we'll get some answers." He yawned. "At least it's not another lindworm."

Odilia shuddered. "I still can't believe you had to face one of those things."

Leonine snorted. "If I hadn't been a dumbass, we might have been able to get away without waking it up. It's a wonder Cimar didn't kill me when it was all over."

"Still can't believe he can turn into a dragon," Everard said, finishing his tea and pouring a second cup, refilling both of theirs before setting it back over the fire. "Only ever heard of that; never thought I'd know someone who could do it." He laughed. "Maybe now that he'll talk to us again, I can see it someday."

"I'm sure he'd be happy to shift for you," Leonine replied. Cimar had always been protective of his dragon form, not wanting to be judged on it or harassed about it, but he'd always been immensely proud too.

The same way Leonine was immensely proud of his magic, for all the trouble and fearful looks it so often brought him. He yawned and set his cup aside, scrubbing at his face to try and wake himself up a bit more.

"Get some rest, Lee," Odilia said. "The gruel won't be ready for a while yet, and you need all the rest you can get with those wounds still healing."

Leonine started to protest, but at their dual glares, lifted his hands in defeat. "Fine. All right. I know when to do as I'm told. Wake me if you sense anything is wrong, I don't care how trivial."

"We will. Promise," Everard replied. "Rest."

Pulling his cloak up around him as a blanket, Leonine stretched out on his bed, enjoying the scent of fresh pine beneath him and the cooking gruel and rabbit around him. Better still was the soft murmuring of his lovers conversing. His lovers. He'd thought he'd lost them forever, but they were his again, hopefully forever, or as close to forever as the goddess permitted.

He groaned as someone shook him gently by the shoulders. "No, a few more minutes."

Odilia's soft, fond chuckle washed over him. "Food's ready, Lee, and then you can go right back to sleep. Come on."

Leonine slowly sat up, shoving his hair from his face and getting his cloak out of the way. Movement caught the corner of his eyes, and he groaned again. "Don't tell me the fucking snow is back."

Everard laughed. "It's like you haven't lived here for years, Lee. Of course it's snowing again. We're lucky it waited this long."

"Why can't assassins work in spring or summer," Leonine muttered, jabbing at the fire before adding more wood to it. Odilia offered a steaming bowl that made his stomach growl, and he gladly took it, barely waiting for each bite to be cool enough to eat.

To his right, Edger said, "Believe me, I would have loved to wait until spring, but the man who hired us insisted it be done at the frost fair."

Leonine cast him a look as he swallowed another bite of food. "So you *are* one of the killers."

"It was Cole what fired the arrows, strictly speaking, but yeah, I was part of the kill team. Five of us in total, with more assistance in cities along the way."

"Who paid you?" Leonine asked. "Why did you take the job? Doesn't really seem your style."

Edger scoffed derisively. "I seriously doubt some pretty boy knight would ever understand."

"I wasn't born a pretty boy knight, you know." Leonine never really talked about his past, not even to Everard and Odilia. Cimar knew his history, of course, but that was it, really. "My parents didn't want another mouth to feed. My foster family decided I was too much work. So did the orphanage and all the other families I tried. I joined the military when I was eight. Sir Cimar found me a few years later. If not for him, I'd probably be dead or worse by now. So try me."

"Lee..." Odilia frowned and fell silent as Everard covered one of her hands with his own.

Edger stared at him intently for a long moment, then gave the barest nod and sipped his tea. "Fine. The short answer is that we wanted out. Gets old being a criminal, you know? Stealing, kidnapping, the occasional murder... eats away at you, and you're always on the run and shit. This job promises enough money we can quit. Buy a house or farm or something, be normal people. That's why. Kill a king that everyone hates and get the life of respectable citizens? Who the fuck wouldn't agree to that? Except this fucking weather screwed us harder than a tax collector seeking bribes." He sighed and drained the last of his tea.

"Tell me about it," Leonine replied. "I hate winter. So they are definitely headed for a ship?"

"The *Fair Morning*. Leaves in six days. Can't tell you where it's going, we were never told, and it didn't really matter to us. *Away* was all that mattered."

Leonine sighed, his orders, his training, and so much more spinning through his head. "For now, let's concentrate on catching up to the rest of your team. Once I have them all, I'll figure out the next step. Now, how about another round for everyone? Tomorrow is going to be a long day."

Odilia served the gruel, and Leonine poured more tea, and they ate the last of the meal in silence, punctuated by whistling wind and the occasional yawn. Everard hauled everything away to clean, and Leonine made sure the fire would last the night.

"Do we need to set a watch?" Odilia asked as Everard returned. "I can take first turn."

"That won't be necessary." Leonine rose and went to the mouth of the cave. Calling up his magic, he willed the snow up and up, until it covered most of the mouth of the cave. With a last surge of power, he turned it into ice, ensuring no one else would be able to get inside without making a great deal of noise. "There. All set. Should keep out the worst of the wind too."

"You really are amazing, Lee," Odilia said, and dragged him into an absolutely marvelous kiss. When she let him go, Everard took his turn, and Leonine was more than a little frustrated that their current company kept him from doing all that he very much wished he could, regardless of how reckless acting on such an impulse would be.

Across the fire, against the back of the cave, Edger was already fast asleep, back to snoring softly.

"What are you going to do, Lee?" Everard asked, voice soft.

Leonine shrugged and spread his hands. "I don't know yet. I really do want to focus on just capturing the rest of the team. After that, I'll sort this mess out. I don't want to make decisions before I have all the pieces. This certainly isn't what I was expecting, though."

Odilia smiled and kissed him again before going to her own bed. "I have every faith you'll make the right decision, whatever it is. We're here for you no matter what."

"I know. Thank you. I'm glad you changed your mind," Leonine replied.

"So are we," Everard said.

They all bedded down, and it was only

minutes before Leonine was fast asleep again.

*~*~*

The snow had stopped when he woke, but to judge by the clouds, it wouldn't stay that way for long. Leonine gulped down the tea that Odilia had made for them, and ate jerky, bread, and cheese as they rode out.

Edger rode with Odilia, a situation that neither Everard nor Leonine was happy about, but there was no choice in the matter. He couldn't walk. Leonine couldn't fight with an additional rider, and Everard's horse couldn't bear the extra weight for as long as they would be traveling.

Thankfully, Edger was clearly in no position to backstab them. Even if he'd wanted to, which Leonine doubted after all he'd confessed the previous night. He wouldn't be able to make any sort of escape, not with his leg and the fact they had all the supplies. If he tried to bolt with Odilia, all he guaranteed was his own death.

"So which of the assholes beat me to a pulp?" Leonine asked.

Odilia cast him a look. "Must we bring that up?"

"Yes," Leonine said. "I intend to repay in kind."

Odilia rolled her eyes.

"Everyone but me and Cole, really," Edger said. "We told them not to be so stupid, to just run, but… Well, me and Cole do this for the money. The rest of them, I always had the impression the money is just a nice bonus. I think the only reason they allowed Cole to make the kill shot was that he was inarguably the best archer of the group, and we were only going to get one chance. If they could have been more… well, hands on… about the matter, I promise you they would have been."

"Doesn't seem like your kind of people," Everard said. "Not that I really know you well enough to speak, but…"

"They're not," Edger replied flatly. "Cole and I usually stick to smaller jobs, the kind that the authorities rarely think is worth the trouble to investigate. On the rare occasions we have been caught and hauled up, we're usually released months early for good behavior, because we're such a minimal threat they'd rather free up the prison cells for more dangerous offenders. Like I said before, though: this job offered retirement money. The kind of money we couldn't have saved up in two lifetimes if we'd never spent a single pence. If we had to put up with some cretins for a few weeks, fine. We've dealt with their sort before." He sighed and stared up at the sky. "Just hadn't counted on busting my leg and being rescued by the royal knight sent to take my head."

Leonine smiled in sympathy. "You certainly could not have had much worse luck. I'd be willing to bet they ditched you not just because they were slowing you down, but on the hope I'd be lazy and satisfied with one head to haul home in this weather, and not trouble myself with the whole set. Unfortunately for them, I'm better trained than that. If I have to be out in this damned weather for days on end, I'm going to make it worth my while."

"Good luck. They're nasty pieces of work, so you'll need all you can get."

"They got me once. They're not going to get me a second time," Leonine replied.

Edger cast him a sideways glance. "Your magic certainly freaks them out. Probably used to that, though. Ain't seen magic like yours ever, only ever heard it sung about, that kind of thing. How'd you get such powerful magic?"

"I was born with it," Leonine said. "I was in the military before I really came to appreciate what an anomaly I was. Probably would have gotten me killed if Cimar hadn't gotten to me first."

"Fascinating."

"Marvelous," Odilia said. "Leonine is amazing in everything he does."

Edger smiled faintly. "I believe you. Even when you three were pretending to be strangers, there was no missing the looks you cast each other when you thought no one else was looking. I'm glad you seem to have fixed whatever was wrong. Cole and I got into a huge fight once, didn't speak for nearly three months. Worst three months of my life. Didn't think he'd take me back. We worked it out, though, and were never that stupid again. Well, until recently." He laughed tiredly. "How did you get the lucky job of hunting us down?"

Leonine smirked. "I'm not telling you anything. You're the one who should be answering my questions."

"So desperation then."

"Hahaha," Leonine retorted.

"He's the best there is, that's why," Odilia snapped. "Watch yourself, or I'll knock you right off this horse and break your other leg."

"Yes, milady," Edger replied with a laugh. "I bet workers and customers alike live in fear of your wrath. Innkeeper, right? That always sounded like a good job to me. So many people to interact with, a place to call your own and care for…"

Everard looked out over the landscape, a pensive look overtaking his face. "We have certainly enjoyed it all these years. We definitely would never have met each other, and later Lee, otherwise." He cast Edger a look. "Why, looking for a job?"

Edger laughed, the sound rippling out across the cold, quiet forest. "Right now, I'm just looking to keep my head where it's at, and to get Cole back safe and sound. I'll see about a proper job when I don't have to worry about staying alive. Just curious how a royal knight comes to be with two innkeepers. Normally all the castle folk wouldn't dare sully themselves."

"Yeah, well, look how well that attitude worked out for His Majesty," Leonine replied. "I think—" he stopped as movement caught his eye. A buck. That would last them days. "I'll be right back. I'm going to catch our dinner for the next several days. Stay here and nobody do anything stupid."

"Fine one to talk, you are," Odilia retorted, but halted her horse, moving to the side of the rode next to Everard. "Be careful, Lee."

"I will." Leonine smiled in parting, then dismounted, drew his bow, and headed off slowly to secure their meals.

# CHAPTER NINE

They reached the city four days later, giving Leonine just over one day to find the bastards, secure Cole, and take care of the others once and for all.

The first order of business, of course, was settling the others. He picked a nice inn, one of those that was strict about who came and went. Ordering two rooms, he got the others settled before sending out for a healer and food.

"I'll be back in a bit," he said, kissing Everard and Odilia. "Keep watch, be careful. If something goes awry, I'll send word."

"Be careful, Lee," Odilia said.

"I will."

She didn't seem terribly convinced, for which he couldn't blame her, but let him go with another kiss, rolling her eyes at his wink.

Snow had resumed falling by the time he stepped outside. Ugh. The next cave he found, he was crawling into it and staying there until the snow was gone.

Leonine headed out, bound for the harbor. Thankfully it didn't take him long to locate the

*Fair Morning,* or its captain, though the man looked less than pleased to see him.

"What business has a royal knight got with me?" the captain asked as Leonine stepped off the gangway and onto the ship proper. Around him, several sailors scattered, off to do work that kept them away from their captain's sudden ire.

"Be at ease, Captain. I'm not here to detain you or delay your departure. I'm just seeking some men who may have bought passage on your ship, believed to be the assassins who murdered His Majesty the King, slain two weeks ago in the midst of the frost fair. Do you have your passenger manifest?"

"Aye." The captain whistled, and when a woman on the far side of the ship turned, bellowed, "Forter, bring me the passenger manifest."

"Aye, Captain!" She vanished from site down a set of stairs, presumably, then reappeared and hastened across the ship, presenting the thick, heavy ledger with a salute.

"Thank you, Forter. Back to task."

She bolted off as quickly as she'd come, and the captain opened the ledger, flipping through pages until the came to the most recent. "What're you seeking?"

Leonine handed of a slip of paper on which he'd copied all the names Edger had given him. "They could be using false names, but these are the ones I was given. Thank you for helping me,

Captain..."

"Tolk." Taking the piece of paper, Tolk skimmed over it and the manifest. "They're all here. Stupid bastards. So they killed the king, eh?" His face said he wasn't sure the men shouldn't be thanked instead of punished, but when he spoke again, he only said, "Anything else I can do for you, Sir Knight?"

"Yes. Do you know where they're lodging?"

"Aye, had to have it in case of a change in departure." He took a pen that was wedged on top of the ledger, flipped over the paper that Leonine had given him, and jotted it down in brusque but elegant hand. "There. Try to keep your trouble away from my ship. We got cargo that can't do much waiting."

"Shouldn't need to trouble you again; this was all I needed. Thank you, Captain, and may the winds favor you."

"Good luck in your quest."

Leonine headed off, trying not to get overly excited. He rode steadily through the streets, mindful of the crowds and patches of ice. He had to stop to ask where the inn in question was located, but after that it took only a few minutes to find it in a seedy corner of the city where everyone gave him suspicious, if not outright hostile, looks before vanishing well out of his sight.

He still wasn't used to the fact it was him,

and only him, that kept causing that reaction. Only a few weeks ago he'd still been a squire, the mostly-invisible shadow attending Cimar. Leonine had thought he'd be inured to the attention, given how long he'd served Cimar, but being the focus made the experience completely different.

He hung well back, not wanting to risk being spotted and causing them to bolt, making his job ten thousand times more difficult.

There were seven in all, which made this tricky. Well, six. His first mission was to get to the seventh one, Cole, and get him to safety. Then he'd deal with the rest.

So for now, Leonine took stock of the buildings surrounding the inn for a suitable place to watch. He finally settled on a bar with an open front, chairs and barrels arranged outside, small fireplace, and an awning, so people could sit outside at all times of the year. Even now, a few people were, smoking more than the fires keeping them warm.

Leonine secured his horse, ordered a pitcher of beer that wasn't watered down and a cup that had seen soap in the last day, and settled into his seat. He thanked the woman who brought him the beer and flipped her a coin to more than cover it, and settled into the uncomfortable seat as best he could.

Hopefully, he wouldn't be waiting long.

In the meantime, he was happy to while

away the time daydreaming of all he'd do when they got home. As a royal knight, he was entitled to his own quarters in the palace, and he could easily pay the additional for larger quarters so Everard and Odilia could come stay with him comfortably whenever they wanted. Horses for them both, so they didn't have to walk everywhere when they didn't want. Would they accept rings if he offered them? He'd never be able to marry them, but…

Not a question he'd be asking anytime soon, not after all that had happened. They could easily change their minds again, decide he really was too much trouble. After the past few days, all the words and touches and kisses… he wanted to believe they were going to stay. Hoped they would stay. But old fears weren't quelled that easily.

He took a sip of the beer, which wasn't as terrible as he'd feared, but still wasn't very good. Across the way, people came and went from the inn, each one more suspicious than the last, but sadly none of them were Cole. Leonine really didn't want to have to go look for him directly, as that would send the others scattering, but if Cole didn't appear by nightfall, he wouldn't have a choice.

What shape was his castle in? His castle. Leonine almost laughed. All he'd wanted from becoming a knight was a place to belong, to never worry about being hungry again, friends, maybe a lover someday. Now he had all of that and an entire castle. Land. If only his parents and everyone else who'd ever thrown him out could see him now.

Movement caught his eye, drawing his attention fully back to the inn, and sure enough, there was the very one he was looking for. Even from here it was easy to tell Cole was tense, unhappy—troubled. Leonine uncurled from his chair and prowled after him, keeping far enough back not to draw attention while ensuring he wouldn't lose sight.

When they were well clear of the inn and anyone who might recognize him, he increased his pace until he was close enough to safely cast out his magic, turning the ground to ice and sending Cole toppling into a snowbank.

Rushing forward, Leonine caught him up and yanked him out of the snow, shoving back his hood as he said, "Hello, again."

Cole looked angry for a split second, and then looked ready to burst into tears. "He's dead, isn't he? Ain't no way you'd have found me unless Edger talked, and ain't no way he'd do that lightly."

"He's fine," Leonine replied. "Well, his leg is still troubling him, and he needs proper food and rest, but my companions are taking care of him as we speak. Come on, I'll take you to him."

At that Cole did burst into tears, and Leonine couldn't not hug him briefly before finally leading Cole back to his horse and getting him up on it.

It took only minutes to ride back to the inn where the others waited, where he handed off his horse before leading an anxious Cole up the stairs and down the hall to the very last room. He knocked three times, then twice more, and the door opened almost immediately. "You're back sooner than expected," Odilia said with a smile. "Come in, come in, the healer just left. Now you're here, I'll go get us proper food."

She kissed his cheek and hastened off, leaving Leonine to lead Cole inside, closing the door behind them. The door hadn't even finished closing before Cole bolted across the room to where Edger was lying in bed, already looking leagues better than when Leonine had left just a few hours ago.

"You're all right, you're all right," Cole said, bursting into tears again as he threw himself at Edger and wrapped tightly around him. "I thought you were dead, you stupid fucking bastard. I thought I'd have to go on without you."

"Never," Edger said fiercely. "Never, Cole. I'm sorry. I don't care about the fucking money anymore. We're done."

"Done," Cole replied, and kissed him. "You're one lucky bastard, and if I wasn't so happy to see you, I'd kill you myself for worrying me to death." He finally drew back enough to look Edger over thoroughly. "Your leg looks leagues better than when I left you."

"Thanks to our mage knight there and his kindliness in paying for a healer—and everything else." Edger sighed, sad and wistful as he said, "I hate we were so close…"

"Forget about it. We've been fine so far, we'll be fine going forward, whatever it takes. I'm just glad you're alive, you clod of mud." He pressed their foreheads together, falling silent.

Leonine left them. He had questions that needed answering, but they could wait a few minutes more. He crossed the room to the window where Everard stood, going easily as Everard pulled him close and treated him to a long, spine-tingling kiss.

"Mmm… what did I do to deserve a kiss like that?" Leonine asked when they finally drew apart. "Tell me so I can get more."

Everard chuckled and kissed him again, leaving Leonine aching. "Just being you, Lee. I'll always be grateful you gave our stupid asses a second chance. You could have anyone in the world, become a prince or king yourself easy."

"No, thank you," Leonine replied. "All I want is to see Odilia become queen of our castle. If I can ever drag her away from the inn," he added with a laugh. "Not that I would. I know how much that place means to the two of you."

"As to that…" Everard's gaze flicked away, resting on Edger and Cole briefly, then shifted back to Leonine. "We've had some thoughts there, wanted to discuss it further with you, but it can wait until this matter is settled. I hope you catch them this time—and without getting yourself nearly killed. I never want to see that again."

"Don't worry, I don't want to experience it ever again." Leonine kissed him one last time before reluctantly drawing back. "Speaking of work, I should get back to it." Returning to Edger's bed, he said, "Hate to interrupt you two, but I need information on the rest of the crew, so I can have done with this."

Cole hesitated, then said, "Why do you care about them? Not that I'd be sorry to see the bastards rounded up, but I was the one who actually did the killing. The only head you need is mine."

"No!" Edger burst out, holding him close. "I'm not letting anyone kill you, I don't care if he did save me."

Leonine lifted his hands, fingers spread. "I'm not killing either of you, all right? The first order of business is to deal with the others. Six in total, though I swear you said the original kill team was five."

"Yeah, we had backup in case something went wrong; they rejoined us in Tesser," Cole replied. "The whole lot should still be at the inn. Haven't left the building, or barely even their rooms, all day. Think they're a bit paranoid after murdering a royal knight."

"Imagine that," Leonine said with a laugh.

"Any nasty tricks I should know about? I'm already aware of some of them."

Before Cole or Edger could reply, the door opened, and Odilia and another woman came in bearing heavily laden trays. Leonine's stomach growled, even though a moment ago he'd have sworn he wasn't that hungry.

Once the trays were settled, the second woman departed, leaving their little group to dine in peace.

"I can't remember the last time I saw so much food and was actually allowed to eat it," Cole said, and beside him Edger looked equally wonderstruck and hungry.

"Eat up," Odilia said in her brisk way. "No good to anyone half-starved. Eat, eat." She took a seat herself, Everard and Leonine sitting on either side of her, the other two taking up the remaining spaces at the table.

As they ate, Cole and Edger shared everything they knew about the other mercenaries. Not much in the end, since it wasn't a group they'd worked with before, but enough that Leonine felt a bit better prepared to face them.

When he'd finished eating, he reluctantly rose and gathered up his weapons and armor, buckling everything into place and bracing himself for the fight ahead. He wasn't stupid enough to think he'd get them without a fight. This time, though, they wouldn't be ambushing him in the snow or while he was highly distracted.

He headed out—but halted when he realized that Everard and Odilia had followed him. "What's wrong?"

"Just want to see you off properly," Odilia said, before dragging him into a kiss that was not remotely appropriate for a hallway. Leonine thought he heard a gasp, followed by a slammed door, but really didn't care as Odilia finished her turn and Leonine was next treated to Everard's ardent attentions.

When they finally let him go, Odilia fondled him in the best, worst way and said, "Hurry back and we'll reward you handsomely, sir knight."

"You're not helping," Leonine said with a groan, and stole a few more kisses before finally forcing himself back to work. "Go away. Stop being brats. I should be back in a few hours at most, but if I'm not back by morning, send Cole to look for me."

"We will," Everard said.

Leonine desperately wanted to go back to kissing them, but he forced himself to turn and leave instead, tucking away the delightful thoughts of his waiting reward so as not to distract himself.

The freezing cold wind finished the job of cooling him off, and by the time he rode out, his mind was entirely on the matter at hand again. The air had gotten even colder, and the clouds above threatened yet another snowstorm. Gods above, he was sick of snow.

Back at the inn where the mercenaries were holed up, nothing appeared to have changed. Securing his horse where he had before so it would draw less attention, he crossed the street to the inn and pushed inside, the wind causing the door to get away from him and slam against the wall. Swearing, Leonine grabbed it and shoved it closed, though the wind fought him so hard that he nearly had to call for help.

Gods, the weather was merciless. Just a couple of hours ago it had almost been pleasant, and now it was beyond miserable, tipping into deadly. They'd be lucky if they were able to make it home before spring thaw at this rate. He'd have to locate a messenger bird and hope it made it through the weather. Well, one problem at a time.

A woman came bustling through the door behind the reception desk. Her eyes widened as she took him in, and when Leonine waved her off, she went right back the way she'd come.

Loosening his sword in its sheath, though in such close quarters a sword wouldn't do him much good, Leonine headed up the stairs, following the directions Cole had given him, until he came to the pair of rooms all the way at the end. According to Cole, the rooms were connected, fairly common in inns like this that were accustomed to housing large groups of people, like families about to set sail.

The windows, according to Cole, were too

small for anyone to climb out of, another feature fairly common to inns like this, so people couldn't slip away without paying. Small windows didn't always stop them, but it certainly made sneaking out more difficult.

Standing in front of the farthest door, Leonine called up his magic, turning the damp, frigid air to ice, sealing the door closed, sticking it firmly enough that all the yanking and pushing in the world wouldn't break it loose.

With that escape route nullified, he turned to the other door. There was a lock on it, and he couldn't imagine mercenaries would be careless enough to leave it unlocked, so that was his next step. Fire would do it faster, but with so much wood around, he didn't want to take the risk, so ice it was.

He froze the lock, inside and out, ignoring the raised voices inside as someone took notice. When it was thoroughly frozen, he removed his sword, sheath and all, and slammed the pommel into the lock.

It shattered like glass, and Leonine drew his sword, discarding the sheath, as he kicked the door open.

Six faces stared at him in a mixture of horror, shock, and anger.

Leonine brandished his sword, calling up flames in his left hand. "Ready for round two, assholes?"

# CHAPTER TEN

Three of them rushed him, knives out, but they fell back immediately as they were suddenly confronted with a wall of scorching flame. Banishing the fire as he surged forward, Leonine stabbed one of them, stole his knife and lodged that in the throat of the next man, and threw the last into two more, sending the new trio into an awkward pile on the floor.

Ice kept them in place, and from there it was child's play to finish them off. One remaining.

"How the fuck are you still alive?" the man demanded. "We saw you die."

"Guess you saw wrong," Leonine replied.

Snarling, the man surged forward, knives out. Leonine brought up his sword to block the swings, but one sword against two knives in close quarters was a laughable comparison. Withdrawing, he abandoned his sword and called up his magic.

"How the fuck do you do that? That shit isn't *real*." The man withdrew, panting heavily. "You're a freaky little bitch, aren't you?"

"Yes," Leonine said, and threw out his

hands as the man came at him again, turning the floor to ice, dodging left as the man slid, stumbled—and slammed face first into the wall. Leonine grabbed him up and snapped his neck, then let the body fall to the floor.

Six down. It was over.

All in all, nothing remotely like his first encounter with them. This time, though, he'd had the advantage, and he hadn't been distracted and acting like a dumbass.

Retrieving his sword, Leonine sheathed it and headed out, going downstairs to send a quick message and pay for the damages to the room and the cleaning that would be required. By the time he was done with that, Cole had arrived, and together they lugged the bodies one by one out into the snow.

"All right," Leonine said as he finished. "Which of these bastards was in charge?"

Cole toed the man at his feet, the one Leonine had killed last, the only one of the six who'd had any chance to put up an actual fight. "This one. Manfred. He took the job, hired all of us, coordinated with the people who were going to pay us." He laughed, though the sound was more tired than amused. "Guess the client got the job done for free. Are you going to track them down?"

"No, it's not worth it. Hardly a secret that literally everyone in this country wanted His Majesty gone. He was getting worse by the day—

the hour, really. Someone just decided to speed things along. Her Majesty wanted the killers for form's sake, and that's what I've done." He drew his sword and removed Manfred's head in two brisk strokes, then knelt and used magic to freeze it solid. Taking Manfred's cloak, he wrapped the head up and bound it with belts taken from two other bodies. "This is all the proof I'll need for Her Majesty."

"And us, I assume?" Cole asked.

"No. Come on, let's get back to our rooms, and we'll finally talk."

Clearly still afraid of what his future held, Cole nevertheless nodded and followed him back to their inn.

Leonine stored the frozen head in the stable near his horse, then ordered mulled wine and food to be sent up to their room before leading the way to it.

Odilia burst out of her chair as she saw them. "You're back already!" She hurried across the room and threw her arms around Leonine's neck, kissing him fervently. "That was much faster than I expected. All this fuss and trouble, and it's over now?"

"It's over now," Leonine said, holding her close, still dizzy with the knowledge that he could do so again. He doubted he'd ever stop being amazed two such wonderful people, a long-established couple at that, wanted him. "I even have a head to prove it, if you want to see it."

That got him a good, solid smack on the chest. "Don't be an ass."

"What? It's true, there really is a head in the snow behind the stable."

Odilia rolled her eyes and pushed him away. "Keep your gory trinkets to yourself, sir knight." She moved to return to the table, but Leonine reeled her back in, pushed her up against the wall, and took a kiss that most definitely was not fit for an audience.

"You're such a brat," she said when they finally drew apart, flushed, lips swollen, eyes sparkling. "Behave now."

"Yes, milady." Leonine withdrew and headed for the table himself, pouring cups of mulled wine, sharing a smirk with Cole, who'd left Edger just as flushed as Odilia. "Where is Everard?"

Odilia smiled as she took a seat, sipping at her wine. "Out spending your money."

Leonine laughed. "Good thing I brought plenty of it. On what, though?"

"Supplies for the return journey. He's determined the returning will be more comfortable than the going."

"I like the sound of that," Leonine said, and drank deeply from his cup before finally turning his full attention to Edger and Cole. "So the only loose threads now are the person who hired you and the two of you. One of those is not solvable without months, even years, of effort. Whoever they are, I've no doubt they've covered their tracks well. More than likely, they're in the castle anyway. So I'm dropping that matter, unless Her Majesty decides otherwise."

"Which leaves us," Cole said miserably. "Executing us would make for a great spectacle and show of power. Even I know that, and I rarely understand anything about you lot."

Before Leonine could reply, the door opened, and he couldn't resist going to greet Everard as enthusiastically as he'd earlier greeted Odilia. "Welcome back."

Everard's eyes gleamed with want and promise. "Good thing I got two rooms, eh?"

"Very good," Leonine replied as he pulled away and put his attention back on the matter at hand. Reclaiming his seat, he said, "No, I'm not dragging the two of you back for execution. In fact, I think you should spend the rest of winter here, give Edger a chance to heal up properly. After that, you can do whatever you want. You're free to go."

They stared at him, mouths agape, and Cole looked near to tears again. "You… you're just going to let us go? Why would you do that?"

"Because it feels like the right thing to do," Leonine replied. "Her Majesty only wants closure, to be able to say she did something to avenge her father, to address the assassination. It would look horribly callous and disrespectful if she did nothing. Why do you think she gave me so much leeway? Alive, dead, or a good explanation. I have two of the three. The rest doesn't matter."

"But…" Cole did start crying then. "I was the one who actually did the killing. I fired the fatal arrows."

Leonine shrugged. "None but the five of us knows that. I'm going to tell one other person, because I want his advice before I turn over Manfred's head, but he can be trusted. So far as I'm concerned, I have the killer in the stable, and the matter is closed, lest Her Majesty bids me pursue it further, which is unlikely."

Edger stared wide-eyed. "That… that is more than we deserve. Far more. We've done nothing to merit that. Why would you…"

Everard smiled, reaching out to touch the back of Leonine's hand. "Leonine is a soft touch, and he's right, this feels like the right thing to do. I mean, let's be honest here: nobody liked His Majesty. He was mean, vindictive, and increasingly violent. He was poisoning everyone and everything around him. Enough people have died; what's the sense in killing two more? As to that…" He reached out and covered Odilia's hand with his own, curling their fingers together. "Odilia and I have been talking… It's time for a change, and you two need a way out of your current situation. How do you feel about learning to run a tavern?"

"What!" Edger, Cole, and Leonine said together. Leonine gaped at them. "You can't be serious. You love that place."

"It's a living," Odilia said. "We liked being together and never having to worry about food or a roof over our head. Now, though… now I've been told I could have an entire castle to prance about if I wanted. Can't be a fancy and run a tavern at the same time, Lee. We'd rather be with you. These two taking over will save us the hassle of locating suitable buyers."

Edger shook his head. "We don't have the money to buy you out. There's no way."

"We don't need the money," Everard replied with a laugh. "Haven't you heard? We've used our wiles on a silly knight who's going to sweep us away to his fancy castle. He has money enough for twenty." He smiled fondly. "He could do better, but he hasn't figured that out yet. Come join us in spring, once it's easier to travel, and we'll get to work. Deal?"

"Um. Yes. Deal," Cole said, wiping his eyes, going easily when Edger pulled him into a hug.

Odilia rolled her head to the door, and Leonine and Everard followed her out, closing the door quietly before slipping into the room across the hall. Leonine had barely closed that door when Everard grabbed him and slammed him against it, holding him easily aloft as he fed at Leonine's mouth like a starving man.

Leonine keened and held fast, kissing back with equal fervor, hooking his legs around Everard's hips. He sank his hands into Everard's hair, keeping him close, one kiss leading into another, until they were panting for air. Everard slowly set him back on his feet, but only so Odilia could take her turn, not ceasing until Leonine's mouth was swollen and faintly bruised from the rush of ardent attention.

"Get out of your layers," she said before biting his ear, then withdrew so she and Everard could do the same. Watching them undress each other, the easy familiarity between them, the looks they gave each other and him, was almost more of a distraction than he could take.

Forcing his eyes away, Leonine got his leather armor and clothes off as quickly as he could manage, taking time only to see the armor was properly put away, consigning everything else to the floor to be dealt with later.

Naked at last, he went back to enjoying the view, groaning and tugging at his cock as Everard moved to stand behind Odilia, bending to kiss the side of her throat as he fondled her breasts with one hand and skated the other hand down to explore further, deeper, making Odilia gasp and push back against him, pretty moans spilling from her lips as he found the spot he'd sought.

Moaning, Leonine moved in to do some touching of his own, taking Odilia's lips as he explored her wet folds himself, his finger right there with Everard's, pushing and teasing, a promise of all that was to come.

Pulling away, licking the taste of her from

his lips, Leonine said, "Someone promised to sit on my face when I was feeling better."

"Then let's move to the bed, sir knight," Odilia said breathlessly, and then shrieked with laughter as Everard scooped her up like a sack of feathers and carried her across the room to the large bed waiting for them. Leonine crawled onto the bed, falling immediately into more touching and kissing, a tangle of limbs, hot skin, and hungry kisses.

Eventually, he was shoved onto his back, and Odilia straddled him with purpose, a gleam in her eyes that he'd never grow tired of. Shifting forward, she settled right over him, baring herself to his mouth, rubbing playfully against his lips in an order to get to work. Bracing his hands on her heavy thighs, he did as told, dragging his tongue along her cunt before plunging his tongue in deep, tasting the musky, salty-sweet of her, lost in her heat, the press of her thighs, the sharp hitches of her breath as she trembled and fought against fucking his face.

She came with a cry just moment later and slowly climbed off, still trembling, chest heaving, skin flushed rose. Leonine sat up, grinning as he used a corner of the sheet to clean his messy face. "I'd call that a good start, hmm, milady?"

"I would agree."

"Put your mouth to work on me, now," Everard growled, pulling him in, reversing their position so he was the one sprawled against the headboard, Leonine between his thighs. Whimpering slightly, his mouth already sore, Leonine nevertheless happily bent to his new task, taking as much of Everard's not inconsiderable cock as he could take, tongue stroking as he hollowed his cheeks and sucked, working further and further, until the tip hit the back of his throat.

Everard moaned and fisted a hand tightly in his hair, and Leonine happily submitted as Everard fucked his mouth with abandon, using none of the restraint Odilia had displayed, withdrawing just enough to plunge deep again, until Leonine was nearly at his limit. Shudders wracked Everard's body, all the warning Leonine got before he sank in deep one last time and came.

Leonine slowly pulled off his cock and heaved for breath as he was able to properly fill his lungs again. He tried to speak, but his throat had taken enough abuse, it wasn't quite ready for that yet. He settled for glaring.

"Sorry," Everard said, grinning shamelessly. He sat up a bit more and dragged Leonine in to straddle his thighs, getting one of those enormous hands around his cock, licking and sucking at his well-used lips as he stroked Leonine off quick and dirty.

Spilling with a moan, Leonine promptly collapsed against Everard's chest. He was hot and sweaty, and so was Leonine, but right then he didn't care. If he really wanted to cool off, he'd just open the window for twenty seconds. "I do enjoy this manner of reward for a job well done."

"We're always happy to give it," Odilia replied with a laugh, sprawling next to them on the bed, idly trailing her fingers over whatever bits of them she could easily reach. "Especially since I think you did most of the work."

Leonine laughed. "I don't consider eating you out while you sit on my face work. Now Everard's cock is a different story."

"Hahaha," Everard said.

Laughter fading, Leonine said, "You've spent a lifetime on that tavern. Do you really want to give it up?"

"It's a living, nothing more," Everard said. "I'm proud of it, of course I am, but we can't split our time between the inn, the castle, and the royal castle. It's too much. If we're going to really and truly be three, then we have to trim some things. Sounds like your new castle will have plenty to keep us occupied, so why not pass the Gold Cock along to people who can devote full attention to it? With that gone, we can spend more time with you whenever you're not out on a mission."

Leonine kissed them in turn, so happy he thought he might burst from it. "I'm so happy you changed your minds."

"You can say 'stopped being so fucking stupid,'" Odilia said with a smile before kissing him again. "We won't be offended."

"You were trying to do what you thought was best. I can appreciate that, even if it *was* fucking stupid." Leonine shifted back just enough he could get a hand around Everard's cock, which was slowly firming again. "Ready for another round already, old man?"

"I'll show you old man," Everard said with a growl, and pushed him backward, sending him sprawling across the bed, head nearly over the edge. Grabbing his thighs, Everard settled between them, huge and hot, rubbing the tip of his cock against Leonine's hole. "Odilia."

"Do I get a turn when you're done?" she asked as she handed over a jar of lubricant, though when she'd had a chance to fetch it, Leonine hadn't the faintest.

He moaned at the idea of Odilia 'getting a turn,' because that meant she'd obtained one of his favorite toys. Before he could ask if that was definitely what she meant, Everard was pushing a thick, slick finger inside him, big enough to stretch him all on its own.

By the time Everard had worked two inside of him, Leonine was already trembling and aching with the need for *more*. "Now, damn it, you know I can take it."

The soft, deep, growly noise that got him sent fresh shivers of anticipation down his spine, and then Everard was pushing inside of him, hard and thick, stretching him not quite to the point of pain, hitching Leonine's breath.

"Ah, sir knight, there's precious little better than being buried balls deep inside you," Everard said, voice raspy with strain. He gripped Leonine's hips and started thrusting, moving slowly at first but quickly gaining speed, until Leonine was forced to grab the edge of the bed to keep from being literally fucked right off it.

He was right at the edge of spilling over when Everard gave an especially hard, deep thrust and said, "Now, now, sir knight, you're not going to come before milady has her fill, are you?"

Leonine whined and whimpered at that. Because of course he wouldn't, but the strain might kill him.

Everard's smug chuckles washed over him, punctuating his hard thrusts, until he finally came with a groan buried deep inside Leonine. "I think we're all blessed you don't charge for this pleasure, Lee. The entire city would go broke."

"Oh, be quiet," Leonine said, already flushed face burning even hotter at the words.

Taking his hands, Everard pulled him up—and then kept going, moving out of the way so Leonine was fully on his hands and knees. Before Leonine could say anything, he felt a much smaller presence behind him, and the hard, cool press of an artificial phallus. He moaned, dropping to his elbows, forehead against the mussed blanket.

Whatever he might have said, if he'd been able to manage it, was lost as Odilia's small but firm hands grabbed his hips, holding him in place as she slowly pushed inside, the phallus completely different from Everard's cock, cool but quickly warming.

"What a sight," Everard said, settling back against the headboard, attention wholly on them, flitting between Leonine's face and Odilia behind him. "Speaking of things I'd go to debtor's prison for…"

Odilia gave a throaty laugh. "Lucky for you then you get it free." She fucked Leonine harder, thrusting in deep, hitting that spot every time, making him scream as he fought to hold on. "Come on then, my champion of dusk and dawn. Spill for me, show me how much you enjoy being at our mercy."

Leonine screamed again as he finally came, adding to the mess they'd already made of the bed. He slumped as Odilia pulled out, too tired abruptly to do anything except lie there and enjoy the sounds of Everard finishing Odilia off, followed by the muffled thump of the phallus being consigned to the floor.

Then he was being shifted about as they dealt with the mussed bedclothes, and only barely awake as they finally settled on either side of him, exactly as they'd done so many times back home, snuggled in the cozy warmth of their room behind the tavern.

Smiling, Leonine finally let sleep have him.

# CHAPTER ELEVEN

They arrived with yet another storm on the horizon, rushing into the Gold Cock chased by a howling wind.

"Look at this place," Odilia said with a laugh. "Feels like we've been gone forever and left only yesterday. I'll get a fire going, scrounge up some food. You get to the matter of baths, Eve."

"Aye, aye, milady."

Leonine left them to it, more intent on getting his message written. Once that was done, he went to find a runner. Normally he'd simply go straight to the castle and speak with Cimar there, but until he'd sorted out the last of his rather complicated mission, he'd prefer no one but Cimar knew he was back.

Thankfully, it didn't take him long to find someone willing to run the message, and when he stepped back into the inn, he was promptly greeted with a kiss and a cup of mulled wine. "No, come back," he said as Odilia slipped away.

She laughed and called over her shoulder, "I have dinner to make."

"I want you not dinner."

"You'll get both, sir knight, never fear."

Grinning, Leonine took his wine and settled at a table close enough to the fire to be warm, but not so close he'd overheat.

He'd just finished the first cup when Everard appeared, carrying a steaming pitcher and a platter of cheese, bread, fruit, and slices of smoked meat. "Isn't much, but it should keep you until we can get a proper meal ready."

"You're my lovers, not my servants, I don't need you waiting on me."

"Good luck telling Odilia not to fuss over you to her heart's content now that we're back in our own domain. Just wait until you give her a whole castle to attend. She might actually find it challenging for a whole year."

"Six months at most," Odilia said as she joined them. "I have some porridge cooking—I hope that's sufficient. Need to do some shopping before we open this place up again."

"Sit down and relax for five minutes, woman. We just got home," Everard said as he pulled her into his lap.

Odilia rolled her eyes. "You two. I do know how to sit in a chair."

"Why let you do that when you can sit on any part of me, and we can all be happy?" Everard said.

Leonine grinned in agreement, but before he could offer a few suggestions about what else would make him happy, the front door slammed open, snatched by the wind, and a familiar figure appeared a moment later on a rush of swirling snow. Brown skin, silvery hair, smaller and slighter than anyone generally expected of a knight: Sir Cimar Vallion, Knight of the Order of the Star and the Order of the Sovereign Rose, Royal Champion, beloved of the Prince Consort, and Leonine's mentor and dearest friend.

"Good evening, all," Cimar said cautiously as he brushed off snow and removed his cloak, hanging it on a hook by the entryway before venturing further inside. "I confess, this is not where I thought you'd asked me to meet you, if you asked me to meet you beyond the castle at all." He flicked his eyes to Everard and Odilia. "Has something changed, then?"

"Have a seat," Leonine said with a laugh. "Yes, something has changed. Would you like some mulled wine?"

Cimar removed his gloves as he sat, setting them aside in an empty chair. "I would love some." He looked again to Everard and Odilia. "If I was harsh with you in error, then I apologize."

"No, don't," Everard said. "We acted foolishly and deserved what we got." He huffed a soft laugh. "Though being so formal did not help us repair matters remotely. We'll leave you two to talk. Let us know if you need anything."

They vanished before Leonine could stop them. "They could have stayed," he muttered as he poured wine for Cimar. "It's good to see you. I know I wasn't gone that long, not really, but this is all..." He waved a hand in the air. "Still very strange."

Cimar smiled. "You look right at home as a full-fledged knight. Tell me why you needed to speak with me in secrecy, and then tell me why you're with those two again, so I may like them once more instead of completely despising them."

"They thought they were holding me back," Leonine replied, in complete disregard for Cimar's orders, and explained all that had happened between him, Everard, and Odilia since setting out on his journey."

Cimar sighed as he finished. "I apologize. You told me not to do anything, but I could not stay from telling them off, for you know I hold you dear. I'm happy they saw sense, and I hope the three of you will be happy going forward. Now tell me the reason for all this secrecy. I can tell you it was a very hard thing to leave behind three curious, nosy lovers to meet with you."

Leonine almost spit out his wine. "*Three.* When I left you had *one*, you dog."

"What can I say, my queen and her handmaiden make persuasive... arguments..." Cimar said with a grin. "Now tell me of the other matter. I did not expect subterfuge from you, especially in the matter of assassins."

"The matter proved to be... strange and complicated."

Cimar's brows rose. "Do tell."

So Leonine did, from his first encounter with Edger and Cole through to coming across Edger dying in a cave, to the violent, bloody end of the matter. "The head is out back, packed in the snow."

"That's nearly as wild a tale as traipsing into a lindworm," Cimar said with a laugh. "If you brought me here to help keep Her Majesty from killing your friends, fear not. I'll take the whole of the tale to her, but I have every faith she'll agree with your actions. She wanted the assassins addressed as a matter of form, and she understands nuance better than most. Come tomorrow to make your formal report, whatever it is you've prepared, and all will be well." He smiled, soft and fond. "You've done well, Leonine. Exemplary, in fact."

Leonine smiled faintly. "I don't know about that, but I'm pleased to have your praise, as ever. Thank you, Cimar."

"Give your lovers my apologies once again, and I'm glad all is well there. I'm going to return before this weather prevents me, but I'll see you tomorrow." Cimar waved him back to his seat when Leonine rose to see him out.

Then he was gone, and Leonine finished his wine before he went in search of his lovers. He found them, as expected, in the kitchen, though he hadn't expected to find them whispering furtively. "What's going on in here?"

"Nothing!" Odilia replied with a smile. "We

absolutely were not discussing your knighting gift. We bought it for you back when you first invited us to your ceremony, and then we felt we obviously weren't allowed to give it to you, and now that we're home again we were discussing when would be the best time. Weren't discussing, rather."

Everard rolled his eyes, and Leonine laughed. "Does this gift involve all of us naked and doing absolutely nothing but staying in bed for a couple of days."

"That was *my* suggestion," Everard grumbled, oofing when Odilia elbowed him. "My suggestion was discarded as too crude for the occasion."

Leonine laughed again. "It's not as though I've ever pretended to have manners. All right then, what's this gift? You have to give it to me now. Not doing so would just be mean."

Odilia rolled her eyes and huffed. "It was meant to be a surprise but *fine*." She thrust her cooking spoon into Everard's chest. "I'll go get it. Don't let the porridge burn."

"Yes, Your Majesty."

She shot Everard a look over her shoulder before she vanished into the back rooms.

"Can we still do the whole stay naked in bed for many hours?" Leonine asked. "All this snow, it's not like there will be much to do, and surely the inn can stay closed for another day or two."

Everard grinned and crooked a finger, and Leonine went immediately, throwing his arms around Everard's neck as he was hauled up that delightful, mountainous body. He tasted like mulled wine, with faint hints of Odilia on his lips, making Leonine moan.

"Oh, you two!" Odilia said as she returned. "What did I say about watching my porridge!"

Leonine laughed as Everard set him back on his feet, laughing harder as Odilia reclaimed her spoon and playfully swatted them both with it.

"Your porridge is fine, woman." Everard rubbed his arm. "Did you bring it?"

"Did you think I went back there to return empty-handed?"

"Oh, just give it to him already."

Sniffing, Odilia turned to Leonine. "It's not much, Lee, but we hope you like it. We're proud of you, and happy for you, and honored to be able to call you ours—especially after how badly we messed up."

Leonine took the small wooden box she held out, running a finger over the symbol burned into the top: three birds sitting on a branch, the mark of a local jeweler. He opened it, revealing a handsome ring: a silver crescent moon and a golden sun, smoothly interlocked. Engraved on the inside was his name and a small heart. "It's beautiful, thank you."

"Nothing like what you can afford now—"

"Shush," Leonine said, and kissed her, cradling her head between his hands, not drawing back until she moaned and squirmed against him. "Must we wait for the porridge to finish?" Leonine asked as he stepped back and slid the ring into place. "Truly, I love it." He liked having a ring they'd given him; he wouldn't have cared if it had been made of paper. "Let me show my thanks."

Before Odilia could say yay or nay, Everard settled the matter by scooping them both up and throwing them over his shoulders as he headed off toward the bedroom, the porridge already removed from the fire so it wouldn't burn.

*~*~*

Leonine had planned to go to the royal castle in the morning to make his report, but as he was getting dressed, a message arrived that he was to come at dinner time, and his formal report could be submitted the next day.

The mystery only increased further when Everard and Odilia started whispering and acting peculiar, slipping away in turns to run errands they wouldn't elaborate on.

He did his best to ignore whatever everyone was plotting by tending to his armor and swords, then his clothes that were desperately in need of washing, and finally helping to get the tavern ready to re-open.

Only as the mid-evening bell rang,

warning him he had an hour until he was due to present himself, did Leonine finally stop and get ready. He'd had to send to the castle for appropriate formal attire, which thankfully required no repairing or other fussing.

His most formal winter tunic was a dark, faintly shimmery gray, trimmed in orange and purple flowers, cinched at the waist with a matching belt of orange and purple stripes, with black hose and high, fur-trimmed black boots. Maybe this was where the smiths had gotten the idea for all the purple and orange in his new weapons and armor. He certainly had no complaints.

When he returned to the dining hall after changing, it was to be greeted by Everard and Odilia in *their* finest, handsomely dressed in dark blue and green respectively, Odilia's hair done up with orange and green ribbons, a silk flower tucked into it on one side, enameled glass earrings dangling from her ears and gleaming at her throat.

Leonine couldn't wait to drape her in jewels and real flowers, fine furs and silks and anything else she wanted. He kissed them both. "I'm getting the distinct impression something is afoot."

"Maybe," Odilia said in singsong tones. "Now let's go, Sir Knight. It wouldn't do to keep Her Majesty waiting."

Leonine offered his arm, and she took it

happily, Everard on Leonine's other side as they headed out. His horse and two others were ready and waiting outside, and though the snow the previous night had not been slight, the roads had been sufficiently cleared that it didn't take much longer than usual to reach the royal castle.

The great hall was even more crowded than usual as they arrived, and Leonine was painfully aware of the hush that swept through as he arrived. Everard and Odilia were escorted away to the high table, which must be giving them heart attacks.

Queen Korena lifted a hand, and behind her two figures rang the gong, ordering silence. Standing, she lifted a cup of wine. "Approach, Sir Leonine of Darting."

Nerves finally hitting him, causing his heart to drum in his ears, Leonine obeyed, walking the length of the great hall to kneel just shy of the dais on which the high table sat. "Your Majesty, I am here to serve."

"Serve you have, honorably and well," Korena replied. "Barely were you knighted when you headed off to hunt down those who murdered my father, our honored late king. You return victorious, despite the weather and other challenges that you faced. We are most grateful. Sir Cimar, if you please."

Leonine started to ask what in the world was going on, but bit the words off at the last, keeping his head bowed only with great effort as

Cimar moved from his position just behind the royal couple and rounded the table, drawing his sword as he did so.

What in the world? He'd already been knighted. Were they doing it again, more formally than the first time?

"Sir Leonine of Darting," Cimar, lightly touching the edge of his sword to each of Leonine's shoulders, "For your service, in this matter and others, Her Majesty grants you the Order of the Moon. Arise."

Leonine rose, eyes wide. That order was reserved exclusively for mage knights of significant skill and valor, the sister to Cimar's Order of the Star for shifters.

Sheathing his sword, Cimar took the pin that a clerk presented and affixed it to Leonine's tunic. There would also be ornamentation for his armor and a ring in the same box. "Thank you, Your Majesty. I am honored.

"The honor is mine, to have such an exemplary knight in my service." She stood again and lifted her cup. "A toast to Sir Leonine, Knight of the Order of the Moon!"

Leonine flushed at the noise that rose up, so much joy and approval directed at *him*.

Better than that was the congratulations he received when he finally took a seat between his lovers.

Fin

About the Author

Megan is a long-time resident of queer romance and keeps herself busy reading and writing it. She is often accused of fluff and nonsense. When she's not involved in writing, she likes to cook, harass her wife and cats, or watch movies. She loves to hear from readers and can be found all over the internet.

meganderr.com
patreon.com/meganderr
meganderr.blogspot.com
facebook.com/meganaprilderr
meganaderr@gmail.com
@meganaderr